A Mighty Adversary

R obin looked over his opponent. He had never seen a taller, larger man. Robin himself was tall, but the stranger towered over him. Robin's shoulders were broad, but this man was twice his size. Still, Robin wasn't about to back down.

"Here is my staff," Robin called when he had finished trimming. "Meet me at the center of the bridge if you dare, and we will fight until one of us tumbles into the stream."

"That's just what I want," said the stranger. He twirled the staff over his head and stepped forward.

READ ALL THE BOOKS
IN THE **wishbone** *classics* SERIES:

Don Quixote

The Odyssey

Romeo and Juliet

Joan of Arc

Oliver Twist

The Adventures of Robin Hood

Frankenstein

*The Strange Case of
Dr. Jekyll and Mr. Hyde*

A Journey to the Center of the Earth

The Red Badge of Courage

The Adventures of Tom Sawyer

Ivanhoe

Wishbone™ Classics

The Adventures of ROBIN HOOD

retold by Joanne Mattern

Interior illustrations by Ed Parker

Wishbone illustrations by
Kathryn Yingling

HarperPaperbacks

A Division of HarperCollins*Publishers*

This is a work of fiction. The characters, incidents, and dialogues are products of the author's imagination and are not to be construed as real. Any resemblance to actual events or persons, living or dead, is entirely coincidental.

HarperPaperbacks *A Division of* HarperCollins*Publishers*
10 East 53rd Street, New York, N.Y. 10022

Cover photographs by Carol Kaelson

A Creative Media Applications Production
Art Direction by Fabia Wargin Design
Edited by Matt Levine

First printing: August 1996

Printed in the United States of America

❖ 10

Introduction

All set to enter a world of action, adventure, drama, and laughs? Then come along with me, **Wishbone.** You may have seen me on my TV show. Often I am the main character and sometimes I am the sidekick, but I'm always right in the middle of a thrilling story. Now, I'm going to be your guide as we explore one of the world's greatest books — THE ADVENTURES OF ROBIN HOOD. Together we'll meet a lot of interesting characters and discover places we've never been! I guarantee lots of surprises too! So find a nice comfy chair, and get ready to read with **Wishbone.**

Table of Contents

ABOUT THE LEGEND
OF ROBIN HOOD

Have you ever heard of Robin Hood? You know, the hero who dressed all in green, was a great shot with a bow and arrow, and robbed from the rich to give to the poor? There are some great stories about Robin Hood—adventures full of action and humor.

The character of Robin Hood is an important part of English folklore—traditional beliefs and stories told by a group of people. Folklore like the legend of Robin Hood was passed down from parents to children to grandchildren. Back about eight hundred years ago, when the stories about Robin Hood got started, people lived very differently than we do today. The King of England gave large pieces of land to a few very rich people, called *lords*. The people who worked for the lords were called *peasants* or *common people*. These peasants were very poor, and they were treated like slaves. They had to work very hard and do whatever the lord told them. They were not allowed to move away or find another lord to work for. In fact, anyone who did this was considered an outlaw and a criminal. Today we call this oppression—the cruel and unjust treatment of people.

One of the worst crimes a peasant could commit was to poach—or kill—the King's deer. Even if peasants were starving or had families to feed, they weren't allowed to hunt deer, or any other animals belonging to the King. If they did, they could be punished by being branded or having their ears or hands cut off.

You can imagine that a lot of peasants weren't happy about the way things were. Then they began to hear stories of an outlaw named Robin Hood who lived in Sherwood Forest and would do anything to help the common folk. If a family was starving or needed money to pay a debt, Robin Hood would give them the food or money that they needed. If a rich man was cheating a poor man, Robin Hood would see that the rich man was punished and the poor man was rewarded. And if someone had nowhere to go, Robin Hood would take him into his band of Merry Men and protect him. Soon stories and songs about Robin began to spread all over England.

Was Robin Hood a real person? No one knows. There *was* a man named Robert of Locksley—Robin Hood's real name in the stories—but no one has been able to find any evidence that he did the wonderful deeds Robin Hood is known for. But one thing is sure—hearing stories about this brave man made people's lives easier. By believing in Robin Hood, people found hope.

Nowadays, the laws we live by are much fairer. People can leave jobs they don't like and fight back against oppression and cruelty. But the stories of Robin Hood and his Merry Men are as thrilling and stirring as ever. So turn the page and become a part of Robin's adventures!

MAIN CHARACTERS

Robin Hood — an outlaw; leader of the Merry Men

Maid Marian — Robin Hood's true love

Little John — Robin Hood's best friend; member of the Merry Men

The Sheriff of Nottingham — Robin's archenemy

King Henry II — King of England

Will Stutely — member of the Merry Men

Arthur a Bland — member of the Merry Men

Will Scarlet — Robin's nephew; member of the Merry Men

Midge — a miller; member of the Merry Men

Allan a Dale — a minstrel; member of the Merry Men

Friar Tuck — a hermit priest; member of the Merry Men

The Bishop of Hereford — a dishonest local churchman

Sir Richard of the Lea — Maid Marian's uncle; a friend of Robin Hood

Queen Eleanor — King Henry's wife

Guy of Gisbourne — an outlaw hired to capture Robin Hood

King Richard of the Lion's Heart — King of England after the death of King Henry

SETTING

Important Places

Nottingham — town in central England

Sherwood Forest — home of Robin Hood and his Merry Men

Locksley — Robin Hood's hometown

London — England's capital and largest city

Finsbury Fields — site of a famous archery contest

1
Robin Becomes an Outlaw

Okay, we all know that Robin Hood was a hero who lived in Sherwood Forest, right? And we know he robbed from the rich fat cats and gave to the poor people, helping them when no one else would, right? But what could have happened to Robin Hood to make him want to live that sort of life?

Our story begins with that very event—the day that Robert of Locksley became...Robin Hood.

It was high noon on a beautiful summer day, and Sherwood Forest seemed to be sleeping. Hardly a breeze stirred the leaves, and the only sounds were the low hum of insects and the soft, sweet song of a bird.

Hidden among the green leaves of the trees, a man stood close by one of the paths that twisted and turned through the woods. He was dressed all in green, and his face was tanned from the sun and the wind. His eyes were as bright and fearless as a hawk's, and his body was tall and strong. In one hand he carried a bow, and a leather pouch filled with arrows hung from his belt.

This man was Robert of Locksley, a freeman of some wealth. Everyone called him Robin Hood. Even though he had his own house and land, he spent most of his time in the forest. He loved the quiet solitude under the trees, where no man was anyone's master and all the creatures ran free. And he loved the common folk who dwelled at the forest's edge much more than he cared for the rich noblemen who treated them so cruelly.

Robin made his way quickly through the forest glades, for he was eager to see the lady he loved most in all the world. Fair Marian was the daughter of a nobleman, but she and Robin had been friends since childhood. They loved each other dearly and swore that neither would marry anyone else.

Today Marian was traveling from her father's house to stay a while at the castle of her uncle, Sir Richard of the Lea. Sherwood Forest could be a dangerous place, and Robin had promised to meet her in the forest and guard her on her journey.

Suddenly Robin heard a noise like the jingling of a horse's bridle. Robin slipped off the path and into the trees, walking so carefully that he didn't make a sound.

Peering through the branches, Robin spotted a band of armed men guarding a knight wearing chain mail. **Chain mail was a type of armor made of links of chain looped together. It was pretty good protection against arrows.** Robin recognized the knight, and his blood ran cold as Robin realized what he was doing there.

"So, Roger de Longchamp," Robin said to himself, "you would seize my lady by force, since you cannot win her by fair means!"

This Sir Roger was one of the cruelest knights in all of England. He ran his castle with an iron fist, and all the peasants who worked there were terribly afraid of him. Sir Roger had asked for the fair Maid Marian's hand in marriage, but her father had refused him. Even though Sir Roger was a powerful man, Marian's father would never give his daughter to someone with such an evil reputation.

Suddenly another armed man ran through the trees to join the company. "They are coming!" he cried. "The lady and her steward are on horseback, and the others are walking. There are nine in all, but they are mere peasants."

"Good!" said Sir Roger. "They will be no match for us. When they come near, I will ride up and seize the lady's bridle. You can take care of the others."

Robin smiled grimly as he slipped an arrow from his belt and fitted it into his bow. He could hear the voices of men coming down the grassy path, as well as the beat of horses' hoofs.

Robin's heart warmed as he saw the beautiful figure of Maid Marian riding toward him. She had pushed her hood back from her face, and her auburn hair gleamed in the sunlight. Beside her rode Walter, the steward of her father's house. **A steward was like the manager of a castle. He was in charge of all the other servants and made sure everything ran smoothly.**

Just then, Sir Roger burst through the trees, followed by his men. Walter bravely pushed his horse in front of Marian's to protect her, but one of Sir Roger's men pulled him from his horse and threw him to the ground, where he lay still.

The other men riding with Marian tried their best to protect her, but they were no match for the armed men they faced. Already, Sir Roger's hands had grabbed the reins of Marian's horse.

Suddenly, there came a sound like that of a giant bee. An arrow flew into the clearing and plunged into the visor of Sir Roger's helmet. The knight gave a deep groan, swayed, and then fell dead on the ground. His men hurried to his side just as another arrow whizzed into the clearing. Instantly they scattered and ran.

Robin Hood stepped out of the trees and hurried over to Marian. "Sweet Robin, I knew you would not fail me," she said, throwing her arms around him. "But I fear Sir Roger's death will cause you great harm."

Robin kissed her hand and pushed back a lock of her hair. "Even if that had been King Henry himself, I would not have stopped my arrow," he told her. "I would do anything to save you from harm."

"But Robin, Sir Roger comes from a powerful family. His brother is a bishop! He will declare you an outlaw, and you will lose your home and all your lands for my sake."

"I knew that sooner or later I would do something that would anger those evil men who think nothing of hurting others. It is done at last, and I am content," Robin said firmly. He kissed Marian's hand once again. "Never fear, my love," he told her. "I will be safe here, and happy. I love the forest more than any place in the world. I will be very happy to make it my home."

"Your happiness is my happiness too," Marian said.

Robin smiled at her. Then he turned to Walter, the steward, who was getting to his feet and shaking his head. "Gather your wits together and take your mistress to safety," Robin told him. "The knight I have slain has evil friends, and they will surely come after us. You know how important Marian is to me. You must take great care of her, for I would not want harm to come to her."

Sir Walter nodded his agreement. "I will take care of her, Robin, never fear." Robin watched as the group rode into the trees.

So Robin was proclaimed an outlaw and his home and lands were taken from him. He could no longer live in his comfortable house, and all his possessions were given to another lord. But the men who had worked on Robin's land were loyal to their master, and they rallied to his side. Many of them went to live with Robin in Sherwood Forest.

Robin took good care of his men, and his men were very faithful to him. Together they did all they could to help the poor and downtrodden. The band soon acquired the nickname "Merry Men," for they took such great joy in life and in helping others.

Soon the people who lived near Sherwood came to praise Robin Hood and his men. Word of his good deeds began to spread all over the countryside, for people knew that anyone who was in trouble could go to him, and Robin would do his best to help.

So there you have it—the beginning of the legend of Robin Hood! Because Robin Hood is a legend, there are many tales about him, his Merry Men, Sherwood Forest, Maid Marian, and other characters you'll soon meet. Turn the page to read one of the earliest stories of Robin Hood!

2
Big Man on a Little Bridge

Robin Hood was always looking for brave, bold men who shared his concern for the poor and wanted to join him. Robin met just such a man—a man who would turn out to be his best friend—while he was out for a walk in the forest one day.

One bright morning, Robin said to his men, "I am going for a walk. You wait here and listen for my signal. If I blow three blasts on my horn, come quickly, for I will need your help."

Robin wandered for a long time through the forest. At last, he turned onto a path that led him to a broad stream spanned by a narrow log bridge. As he drew closer, Robin saw a very tall stranger coming from the other side. The man was big and strong, with long, curly, dark hair and a thick beard. Robin walked faster, but so did the stranger. Each wanted to be the first to cross the bridge, but they ended up getting there at the same time.

"Stand back," said Robin, "and let the better man cross first."

"Stand back yourself," answered the tall stranger, "for I am the better man."

"We shall see," said Robin. "If you don't step aside, I shall show you how we shoot arrows in Sherwood Forest."

"You are a coward," announced the stranger. "You stand there with a bow and arrows to shoot at me while I hold nothing but a quarterstaff to defend myself."

A quarterstaff is a long, thick length of wood.

"No one has ever called me a coward!" Robin snapped back. "I will lay my bow and arrows aside and cut my own staff, if you are brave enough to face me then."

"I will look forward to it!" announced the stranger.

Robin stepped off the bridge and cut a strong, straight staff of oak about six feet long. He came back trimming twigs and leaves from the staff while the stranger waited for him, leaning upon his own staff and whistling.

Robin looked over his opponent. He had never seen a taller, larger man. Robin himself was tall, but the stranger towered over him. Robin's shoulders were broad, but this man was twice his size. Still, Robin wasn't about to back down.

"Here is my staff," Robin called when he had finished trimming. "Meet me at the center of the bridge if you dare, and we will fight until one of us tumbles into the stream."

"That's just what I want," said the stranger. He twirled the staff over his head and stepped forward.

Never did any two knights meet in a such a fight as these two. Robin stepped up and swung at the stranger's head. The blow would have sent the man straight into the water, but he managed to turn away in time.

The two fought for an hour. Many blows were given and received, until both men were sore and bruised, but neither would give in. Now and then they stopped to rest, and each thought he had never seen such a worthy opponent.

At last Robin gave the stranger such a blow upon the ribs that the man almost fell off the bridge. But he regained his balance and thwacked Robin over the head. Blood ran down Robin's face.

Then Robin grew angry. He swung at the stranger with all his might, but the man warded off the blow. Then he hit Robin so hard that Robin fell head over heels into the water.

"Where are you now, good lad?" the stranger called, roaring with laughter.

"Oh, drifting away with the tide," Robin sputtered. He couldn't help laughing himself as he waded to the bank. "You are a strong man. My head is humming like a hive of bees."

"You fought well and took your beating like a brave man," the stranger complimented Robin as he helped him out of the stream.

When Robin was back on dry land, he put his horn to his lips and blew three notes. Soon the forest rustled with the sound of footsteps, and a score of Merry Men, all clad in Lincoln green, burst onto the path. **Lincoln is a city in England where a type of green cloth was made. The color became known as Lincoln green.**

"Good friend," cried Will Stutely, one of Robin's men, "why are you wet from head to foot?"

"This stout fellow has tumbled me into the stream and given me a beating besides," Robin said.

"Then he shall not go without a dunking and a beating himself!" cried Will. "Have at him, lads!"

Will and the other men leaped upon the stranger, but they found him more than ready to fight. The stranger struck right and left with his staff so that even though he finally fell, many of Robin's men were rubbing bruises before the giant was overcome.

"Stop, stop!" Robin cried, laughing so hard his sides ached. "He is a good man." Robin turned to the stranger. "My name is Robin Hood. I live here in the forest with my men."

"Robin Hood!" the tall man said in surprise. "I have heard a lot about you and your good work."

"Will you stay with me and be one of my band?" Robin asked. "You shall share whatever good befalls us and be my own right-hand man."

"I don't know," the stranger replied. "If there is any man here who can shoot better than I can, I will think about joining you."

"Will Stutely, cut a piece of white bark four fingers wide and set it on yonder oak," Robin ordered. "Now stranger, hit that fairly and you may call yourself an archer."

The stranger chose a bow from one of Robin's friends and stepped up to the mark. Then he sent an

Being someone's right-hand man means that you are his closest companion and second in command.

arrow so straight down the path that it split the mark in the very center. "Ha!" he cried. "See if you can match that!"

"That is a good shot indeed," said Robin. "Maybe I cannot match it, but I will try my best to shoot even better."

Taking up his own bow and nocking an arrow with care, Robin shot with his greatest skill. **Nocking an arrow isn't like knocking on a door. It means to place an arrow against the bowstring and get ready to shoot it.** The arrow flew so straight and true that it hit the stranger's arrow and split it into splinters. All the men leaped to their feet and shouted for joy that their friend Robin had shot so well.

"I never saw a shot like that in all my life!" cried the stranger. "I will be your man forever."

"Then I have gained a good man this day," Robin said. "What is your name?"

"Men call me John Little," answered the stranger.

Will Stutely, who loved a good joke, spoke up. "I do not like that name," he said to the huge stranger. "You are little indeed, and so we shall call you Little John."

Robin Hood and his men laughed so hard that the man grew angry. "If you are making fun of me," he said to Will, "you will have sore bones, thanks to me."

"No, good friend, don't be angry," Robin told him. "Little John it shall be. Come along with me."

The men plunged into the forest and brought

Little John to their home deep in the woods. Here they had built huts of bark and branches near a great oak tree. Robin settled under the tree as his men roasted a fat deer. Robin Hood placed Little John at his right hand, and the band had a feast to welcome their new member.

As you can see, not just anyone can join Robin Hood and his men. You have to prove your bravery and strength first! Little John will turn out to be a good friend and a loyal member of the band, and he'll share many adventures with Robin Hood. Let's see what happens next!

3

The Great Archery Contest

The common folk loved Robin and his men because of their kindness and protection, but the Sheriff of Nottingham wasn't happy about an outlaw running around in the forest, disobeying the King's laws. In fact, the Sheriff would do anything to capture Robin, as we'll see in this chapter.

The Sheriff was the most hated man in Nottingham. Everyone was afraid of him because he punished even the slightest crime with a harsh penalty. Also, the Sheriff was in charge of collecting taxes for the King. If a poor peasant couldn't pay his tax—and many of them could not—then the Sheriff did not hesitate to throw him into jail or take away his home and all his possessions.

To the Sheriff, Robin and his men were simply a band of lawbreakers. Nothing made him angrier than the thought of Robin and his men living in Sherwood Forest and doing whatever they liked. It also embarrassed him that he could not catch Robin no matter how hard he tried.

"I know I am no match for Robin in Sherwood Forest," the Sheriff said to himself one day. "But if I could trick Robin into coming to Nottingham, then I could lay my hands on that outlaw so firmly that he would never get away again!"

Then the Sheriff had an idea. "I will proclaim a great shooting match and invite all the archers to compete for a grand prize," he said. "Robin is so proud that he will never be able to pass up a chance to show off his skill! And once he is in my clutches, I'll end his days of helping those peasants and disobeying my laws!"

So the Sheriff sent messengers north and south, east and west, to proclaim the great shooting match throughout the land. The prize would be an arrow made of pure gold.

When Robin Hood heard about the contest, he gathered his men around him. "I would like one of us to win that golden arrow," he said. "Not only is it a wonderful prize, but it will allow us some sport at the expense of our good friend, the Sheriff."

Just then, one of Robin's men said, "I have heard all about this shooting match. I also heard that this is a trap to catch you, Robin. You'd best stay here in the greenwood."

"What?" Robin shouted. "Shall I let it be said that Robin Hood and his men were afraid of the Sheriff? What you've told me only makes me want that prize even more. But we shall meet the Sheriff's trickery with our own. We will dress as friars and peasants and beggars to fool the Sheriff and his men, but each of us will carry a good bow or sword, in case we should need them." All of Robin's men agreed that this was a good plan.

Nottingham was a fair sight on the day of the shooting match. Never had such a brave and strong company of men been gathered together, for the very best archers in England had come to the match. Benches had been set up along the meadow for the rich people to sit on, while the poor settled down on the grass. At the far end of the field was a brightly decorated grandstand where the Sheriff would sit. The air was filled with laughter and excited talk.

The Sheriff rode in on a beautiful white horse and took his place in his seat. He was a tall, powerfully built man, and he cut a fine figure in his elegant clothes. But despite his handsome appearance, the crowd booed as soon as they saw him. He glared at them with a fierce, angry expression on his face.

The Sheriff's herald blew upon his silver horn and proclaimed the rules of the contest. "Each man will shoot one arrow from that mark," he said, indicating a line about one hundred fifty yards from the row of targets which had been set up. "The ten best will shoot again, receiving two chances this time. The three that do best will shoot again. Each will have three chances. He who shoots the best will win the prize."

Everyone cheered as the archers stepped forward. The Sheriff looked hard at the group, but he did not recognize Robin Hood or any of his men. "He may still be there," the Sheriff said to himself. "I will wait until the field is cut to ten men, for I am sure he will be among those ten."

The archers fired off their arrows in turn, and the ten best men were chosen. Of these ten, six were known throughout the land. Two others were from the north of England, and another was a tall man from Lincoln. The last man was a dark-haired stranger dressed in tattered scarlet who wore a patch over one eye.

"Do you see Robin Hood among those ten men?" the Sheriff asked his men-at-arms. They shook their heads no.

The Sheriff slapped his thigh in anger. "Robin Hood is a coward, then, if he dares not show his face here today!" he shouted.

After a brief rest, the ten archers stepped forward to shoot again. Each man shot two arrows. The crowd watched in silence until the last arrow was loosed. Then everyone cheered and waved their caps at such marvelous shooting.

Now only three men were left. Gill o' the Red Cap and Adam o' Tamworth were two of the best known archers in England. The third man was the tattered stranger in scarlet.

Gill shot first. His arrow flew straight and landed almost exactly in the center of the target.

The Sheriff clapped loudly. "That was an excellent shot!" he cried.

Next it was the turn of the tattered stranger. The crowd laughed at his shabby clothes and the patch over his eye, but his arrow was closer to the center than Gill's.

The Sheriff shouted his approval along with the crowd. Then Adam o' Tamworth stepped forward. His arrow lodged close beside the stranger's.

The three men shot a second time, and then a third. Gill's third arrow was the closest to the center—until the stranger sent his own arrow flying. His arrow knocked a feather from Gill's arrow and lodged in the very center of the target.

Adam o' Tamworth stepped forward. "I have been shooting for over forty years," he said, "but I will shoot no more this day, for no man can match that man's skill."

Then the Sheriff stepped forward and presented the golden arrow to the stranger. "Here, good fellow," he said. "Take your prize, for you have earned it. What is your name?"

"Men call me Jock," said the stranger.

"Jock, you are the finest archer I have ever seen. I trust you are even better than that coward Robin Hood, who dared not show his face this day. Will you join my service?"

"No, I will not," said the stranger firmly. "No man in England shall be my master—especially a man as evil and cruel as you!"

The Sheriff trembled with anger. "Get away from here before I have you beaten for your rudeness!" he shouted. He turned on his heel and stalked away.

• • • • •

That same day there was a merry feast in Sherwood's depths. Everyone gathered around a man in tattered scarlet with a patch over one eye, who sat under the greenwood tree and held the golden arrow in his hand. Amid shouts and laughter, the man took the patch from his eye and stripped off his scarlet rags. It was Robin Hood himself who had won the prize. "I only wish the plant dye I used to darken my hair could be removed as easily as these clothes," he said, laughing.

After the feast, Robin Hood took Little John aside and said, "It angers me that the Sheriff called Robin Hood a coward for not showing up today. I would like him to know who really won the golden arrow, and that I am not the coward he takes me to be."

"Let me and Will Stutely go to the Sheriff," said Little John. "We will send him news of all this by a messenger he does not expect." Robin agreed.

That evening, as the Sheriff dined in his great hall at Nottingham, something flew through the window and rattled down among the dishes on the table. One of the men-at-arms picked it up and brought it to the Sheriff. Everyone could see it was an arrow with a paper rolled around the shaft.

The Sheriff opened the paper, and his face grew red with anger as he read the words aloud:

"Now Heaven bless Your Grace this day,
Say all in sweet Sherwood,
For you did give the prize away
To merry Robin Hood.

"Why that rotten, sneaky, lying..." the Sheriff sputtered. He grabbed his dinner plate and flung it across the room, narrowly missing a servant's head. "I'll catch him yet and make him pay for his tricks!"

Ah, I love a good poem—and a good joke! The evil Sheriff of Nottingham has learned what happens when a person underestimates Robin. But the Sheriff is persistent, and now he's angry. Robin and the Merry Men haven't heard the last of him, as we'll see in the next chapter!

4

Robin to the Rescue

When the Sheriff of Nottingham realized that his trickery could not capture Robin Hood, he decided that using force was the answer. So he called his men-at-arms together and said, "All of you go into the forest and hide yourself in different places. Lay in wait for Robin Hood and do your best to capture him. If any one of you finds too many men against him, sound your horn so the others can come to your aid. This way we shall take the bold Robin Hood!"

The Sheriff added, "The man who brings Robin Hood to me, dead or alive, will receive a reward of one hundred pounds. And he who brings me any of Robin's men, dead or alive, will receive forty pounds. Now, be bold and be crafty—and bring me Robin Hood!"

So the Sheriff's army went into Sherwood Forest. There wasn't a man among them who didn't want to be the one to capture that bold outlaw or one of his Merry Men. For seven days and nights they hunted through the forest. But a friend had warned Robin of the Sheriff's plan, and he and his men hid themselves so well that the army never saw a single man in green.

On the eighth day, Robin called his men together. "Which of you will go and find out where the Sheriff's men are now?" he asked.

A great shout arose as each man waved his bow and said he would be the one to go. Robin was proud of them. He said, "You are all brave and loyal men. I choose good Will Stutely, for he is as sly as an old fox."

Will jumped up and laughed for joy at being chosen, for he, like all of the men, would do anything for Robin. He dressed quickly in the disguise of a friar and hid a sword under his gown where he could quickly lay his hands on it. Then he ventured forth on his quest.

Will came across two bands of the Sheriff's men as he made his way through the forest, but he did not stop to talk to them. Instead, he made his way to a tavern called the Sign of the Blue Boar. **A tavern is a place where food and drink are served.** Here he found a band of the Sheriff's men talking loudly together. Will settled down in a corner to listen to them.

As Will sat with his head bent so no one would recognize him, a house cat padded across the room and rubbed against his knee, pushing up the friar's robe. Will quickly yanked it down again, but not before one of the Sheriff's men saw a flash of Lincoln green beneath Will's robe.

The soldier turned to Will and asked, "Where do you go, holy friar, on this hot summer's day?"

"I go as a pilgrim to Canterbury Town," Will answered, speaking gruffly so no one might recognize his voice. **Many people journeyed to the English city of Canterbury to pray at the great church there.**

"Do pilgrims to Canterbury wear Lincoln green beneath their robes?" the soldier asked. "I think you are really a thief and a member of Robin Hood's band. If you move so much as a finger, I will run you through with my sword!"

The soldier flashed his bright sword and leaped upon Will, thinking to take him by surprise, but Will was holding his own sword tightly beneath his robe, and he drew it out before the soldier could reach him. He struck the soldier so hard that the soldier reeled and fell. Then the other men rushed upon Will.

Will swung his sword right and left. "Get away from me or you will lose your life!" he shouted. But despite his brave words and deeds, Will could not hope to win against so many opponents. The soldiers quickly knocked him down and tied his arms and legs with sturdy rope. "You'll be sorry!" Will shouted at them. "Robin Hood will come to save me!" But his captors only laughed at Will as they brought their prize to the Sheriff.

Will Stutely is in a tight spot! Do I smell a rescue on the way?

Robin was sitting beneath the greenwood tree when a young woman who worked at the Blue Boar came running down the path, guided by one of the Merry Men. She was a good friend of the band and often visited them in the forest. Today she looked so upset that Robin knew she was bringing bad news.

"Will Stutely has been captured by the Sheriff's men!" the woman cried when she saw Robin. "They have taken him to Nottingham, and he will be hanged at sunset tomorrow!"

"Not if I have anything to say about it!" Robin replied. He blew three blasts on his horn, and soon all his friends hurried to join him.

"Our dear companion, Will Stutely, has been taken by the vile Sheriff," Robin told them. "It is up to us to risk our lives to save him, just as he would risk his life for us!"

"Yes!" all his men shouted.

"Now," Robin continued, "if there be anyone here that cares not to risk his life, let him stay within the forest, for I will force no man to do my will. But know this: I will bring Will Stutely back or I will die with him."

"Good Robin," said Little John, "do you think any one of us would not risk life and limb to save a friend in need?" The Merry Men all shouted their agreement. Not one among them wanted to be left behind.

The next day, Robin and his men made their way to Nottingham. They joined the crowd gathered there, making sure to stay near the gallows where Will Stutely would be hung.

Presently the castle gates opened and the Sheriff's

men-at-arms rode forth with a great noise and clatter. The Sheriff rode before them, clad in armor. In the midst of the guards, riding on a cart with a noose around his neck, was Will. He was pale and his hair was matted with blood from the fight, but he spoke up bravely nevertheless.

"Give me a sword, Sir Sheriff," Will said, "and I will fight you and all your men until my life is gone."

"No, you shall have no sword," the Sheriff told him coldly. "You shall die a mean death, just as a thief and outlaw deserves."

"Then untie my hands and I will fight you and your men with my fists alone!" Will cried. But the Sheriff only laughed at him.

"You are a coward," Will shouted. "If my friend Robin Hood ever finds you, you will pay dearly for this day's work. Don't you know how he laughs at you? You are a joke to every brave man in Sherwood."

"Then I will make a joke of you today, and a sorry joke you will be!" the Sheriff replied angrily.

The cart rumbled onward through the crowd. At last they came to the gallows. Will looked out at the fair country, the green hills and dales, and the sun slanting down on the fields and farms. He heard the birds singing and the sheep bleating. Will's eyes filled with tears at the thought that he was about to leave this world. But when he blinked the tears away, Will's heart leaped with joy, for he saw Robin Hood and his friends standing at the front of the crowd.

"Stand back!" shouted the Sheriff's men as the

crowd pushed around him. But one huge man pushed his way right up to the cart. It was Little John.

"Stand back yourself," the giant shouted, and whacked one of the soldiers over the head. Then Little John leaped onto the cart and quickly cut the ropes binding Will's arms and legs. "I will die with you if I must," the big man said, "for I could not ask for better company."

"That is one of the outlaws!" the Sheriff shouted at his men. "Take him!" The Sheriff spurred his own horse toward Little John, but the big man ducked under the horse and out of the way.

"Good Sheriff," Little John said, "I must borrow your sword." He yanked the weapon out of the Sheriff's hand and passed it to Will.

"How dare you steal my weapon!" the Sheriff sputtered, but Little John ignored his angry words.

"Stand back to back with me and defend yourself," Little John told Will. "Help is on the way!"

Just then an arrow whistled within an inch of the Sheriff's head. Robin Hood and his men rushed forward to the rescue. The sound of clashing swords and flying arrows filled the air. Robin and his men were winning the battle!

"Back, back!" the Sheriff shouted. "We are all dead men if we stay!"

Robin Hood and his men let the Sheriff and his soldiers ride away, sending a flight of arrows after them to speed them along.

"You will never catch bold Robin Hood if you do not dare to meet him face to face!" Will shouted after the Sheriff, but the Sheriff only spurred his horse to a faster pace.

Then Will Stutely turned to Little John and the tears ran down his cheeks. "Little John, you are my own true friend, and I love you more than anyone in the world," he said. Little John could not answer, for he was crying too. **Group hug!**

Robin Hood gathered his men together and they traveled back to Sherwood. Meanwhile, the Sheriff was ashamed at what had happened that day, and he was angrier than ever at Robin's boldness. "I have never hated a man as much as I hate Robin Hood," he said. "He disobeys my laws and makes a fool of me! I won't allow it! Robin Hood may have won this time, but someday I will get my revenge!"

Hooray for the home team! Will Stutely is rescued, and the Sheriff is sent scurrying back to Nottingham. Funny thing, though...I don't think Robin is finished having fun at the Sheriff's expense. Wait till you see what Robin does next—right under the Sheriff's nose!

5
The Merry Butcher of Nottingham

Robin Hood often thought of other ways to help the poor than simply giving them money. In this next tale, you'll see what I mean....

One fine day Robin set out for the edge of Sherwood. As he rambled along the sunlit road he met a young butcher riding in a new cart with cuts of meat hanging from its sides. The butcher whistled as he rode along, for the day was warm and sweet and he was happy to be going to market.

"Good day, jolly fellow," Robin called to him. "You seem happy this morning."

"Why shouldn't I be?" answered the butcher. "I am healthy and strong, and I will marry my sweetheart next Thursday in Locksley."

"Locksley," repeated Robin. "I know that beautiful town very well, for I was born there. Where are you going with your meat, my good friend?"

"To the market in Nottingham to sell it. But tell me, if you are from Locksley, what is your name?"

"Men call me Robin Hood."

When the butcher heard Robin's name, he grew alarmed. "Many a time I have heard your deeds sung and spoken of," he said. "Please don't take advantage of me, for I am an honest man and I have never troubled anyone."

"Heaven forbid," said Robin. "I would never take from a fellow like yourself. But please, for what price would you sell all your meat and your horse and cart?"

"The meat, cart, and horse are valued at four marks," the butcher replied.

Robin Hood pulled the money pouch from his belt and said, "Here are six marks. I would like to be a butcher for the day. Will you sell me your goods for six marks?"

"Yes!" cried the butcher, overwhelmed by Robin's generosity.

So Robin put on the butcher's apron and his cap. Then he climbed onto the cart and drove into Nottingham.

Robin entered the part of the market where the butchers stood and found the best spot he could. Banging his cleaver on the boards of the cart, he called out his prices. "I will sell three pennyworths of meat to a fat friar for sixpence, for I do not want his business. To a businessman I will charge threepence, for I do not care whether he buys from me or not. I will sell three pennyworths to a housewife for one penny, for I like her business well. And to a bonny lass, I will charge nothing but one sweet kiss, for I like her business best of all."

What a bargain!

Everyone crowded around, laughing at Robin's words, for they had never heard of such a thing, but when they came to buy, they found that Robin did exactly as he said. He charged a housewife only one penny for meat that cost three pennies elsewhere, and he did not charge widows and poor women anything at all. And when a pretty young girl came and gave him a kiss, Robin laughed in delight and gave her meat for free.

The poor people of Nottingham flocked around Robin's stand, for here they could buy plenty of meat for very little money. Robin sold his meat so fast that no other butcher could sell anything, and many people who would have gone hungry went away with their arms loaded with meat.

The other butchers began to talk among themselves, wondering who this strange man could be. "He must be a rich man who has money to spare," one of the butchers said. The others agreed that this must be true.

"The Sheriff has asked the Butcher's Guild to feast with him today," said one of the butchers to Robin as the morning grew late. "Will you come and dine with us?" **In Robin Hood's day, merchants and craftsmen belonged to a guild, or an association of people in a particular business, just as they do today.**

Robin agreed. He sold the last of his meat, closed up his stall, and went with the others to the great Guild Hall where the feast was to be held.

The Sheriff was already seated at the head of the

table when Robin arrived. Some of the butchers sitting near the Sheriff whispered to him, "That young man sells his meat for a kiss to any pretty girl. He must be a rich man who intends to spend his money as fast as he can."

Then the Sheriff called Robin to him, not knowing him in his butcher's apron and cap, and made him sit at his right hand. **Just like being called someone's right-hand man, sitting at someone's right hand was a great honor. It meant you were the most important guest.** The Sheriff loved to meet rich people—especially if he thought he could get some of their riches for himself.

The Sheriff talked and joked with Robin all through the meal. "You are a jolly fellow, and I like you very much," he said.

"Yes," said Robin, laughing. "I know you like jolly fellows. Didn't you have jolly Robin Hood at your shooting match, and didn't you award him a bright golden arrow for his own?"

The Sheriff glared at him. "Come, let us enjoy our meal," Robin shouted. "Don't look so glum, Sir Sheriff. You might catch Robin Hood one day, if you shake the dust from your brain."

The Sheriff laughed weakly, as if he didn't think Robin's joke was very funny. "You are certainly a happy lad," he said stiffly. "You must have many herds of animals and acres of land, since you spend your money so freely."

"Yes, I do," Robin said. "My brothers and I have

more than five hundred beasts in our care, but we cannot sell a single one of them. As for my land, I have never asked how many acres I have." **The animals Robin is talking about are the deer in Sherwood Forest, and his land is the forest itself. He's making a joke, but the Sheriff doesn't know what he means!**

The Sheriff's eyes twinkled. "If you cannot sell your herds, perhaps I can buy them from you. How much do you want?"

"At least five hundred pounds," Robin replied.

"No," the Sheriff said slowly, as if he were thinking hard. "Five hundred pounds is too much. I will give you three hundred."

"What!" cried Robin, outraged. "You know that so large a herd is worth at least seven hundred pounds, yet you think to buy them from me for only three hundred?"

The Sheriff gave Robin such a harsh look that the young man quickly backed down. "All right, I will take your offer, for my brothers and I need the money," Robin said.

"I will bring the money today," the Sheriff promised. So the bargain was closed, although the other butchers whispered among themselves that it was wrong of the Sheriff to cheat a youth that way. But Robin wasn't worried. He had it in his mind to play a great trick on the Sheriff—and teach him a lesson for being so greedy.

That very afternoon the Sheriff mounted his horse and joined Robin Hood, who was waiting for him in the courtyard. He had sold his horse and cart to a trader for two marks. The Sheriff rode into Sherwood with Robin running beside him. The two laughed and joked like old friends, but the Sheriff was thinking, *That joke you made about Robin Hood will cost you, young fellow, for I will make a tidy profit selling your animals for seven hundred pounds!*

As they rode into Sherwood Forest, the Sheriff looked about nervously. "May Heaven and its saints protect us from that outlaw Robin Hood," he said.

Robin laughed. "Set your mind at rest. I know Robin Hood well, and you are in no more danger from him this day than you are from me."

The Sheriff frowned. "I do not like it that this fellow is friendly with an outlaw such as Robin Hood," he said to himself. He was beginning to wonder if coming into Sherwood Forest with this man had been such a good idea after all. Did the fellow mean to harm him?

The path turned sharply as they rode deeper into the forest, and a herd of deer ran in front of them. "Those are part of my herds," Robin told the Sheriff. "How do you like them?"

The Sheriff pulled back on his reins to stop his horse, for Robin's words upset him. "I don't like your company," he said. "I think it would be best if you go your way and let me go mine."

Robin grabbed the Sheriff's reins. "Oh, no," he said. "Stay a while, for I would like you to meet my brothers." With that, he blew on his horn. Soon Little

John and some of Robin's other friends came hurrying down the path.

"What would you have us do, Robin?" Little John asked.

"Robin!" the Sheriff shouted. "You mean *you* are Robin Hood?"

"None other," Robin said, taking off his cap and apron. Then Robin turned to Little John. "Can't you see that I have brought fine company to feast with us today?" he asked. "It is our good friend, the Sheriff of Nottingham."

Little John led the Sheriff's horse deeper into the forest, with Robin and the other men marching beside him. The Sheriff was angry and worried now that he realized who the butcher really was. *These outlaws will take my three hundred pounds, and maybe my life as well, for I have plotted against their lives more than once!* he thought nervously.

At last they came to the great oak tree at the center of the forest. Robin settled down beneath the tree and placed the Sheriff at his right hand. "Bring forth the best meat and drink we have," he told his men, "for we will have a great feast tonight."

While bright fires crackled and the air filled with the delicious smells of roasting deer, Robin Hood's men entertained the Sheriff with a bout of quarterstaffs and an archery contest. Despite his worries, the Sheriff relaxed and began to enjoy himself, for he liked nothing better than watching fine sports. Afterward, everyone sat down and feasted merrily together until the sun was low and the moon glimmered between the trees.

Finally, the Sheriff stood up and said, "I thank you all for the entertainment and the fine meal you have given me this day. But the shadows grow long, and I must get away before darkness comes and I lose myself in the forest."

Robin Hood and his men also stood up. "You may go if you like," Robin said, "but you have forgotten one thing. We keep a cheery inn here in the greenwood, but whoever comes here must pay for his meal."

The Sheriff laughed nervously. "We have had a fine time together today. I would gladly give you a few pounds."

"Oh, no," said Robin. "I would not treat you so cheaply as that. I think your meal was worth three hundred pounds. Don't you agree, my friends?"

Robin's men shouted their agreement. The Sheriff's face grew red with anger. "I will not pay such a price!" he roared.

"Sir Sheriff, I would not harm you, but there are those here who do not like you very much," Robin warned him. "Look, there is Will Stutely, who bears no love for you. You'd best pay me the price I've asked for, or things may not go well for you."

The Sheriff grew pale at Robin's words. Slowly, he pulled out his fat money pouch and threw it on the ground.

"Count the money and see that it is right, Little John," Robin ordered.

Little John counted the money and found that the pouch did indeed hold three hundred pounds in silver and gold. To the Sheriff, the clink of each coin was like a drop of blood from his veins. When he saw it all counted out on the ground, he turned away and silently mounted his horse.

"Let me send one of my men to guide you out of the forest," Robin offered, for his camp was so deep in the woods that no one but the Merry Men could find it without help.

"No, I can find my own way," the Sheriff snapped, although he wasn't at all sure he could.

"I will lead you myself," Robin said, "for we wouldn't want you to get lost, now would we?" He brought the Sheriff's horse to the main path out of the forest. Then he said, "Farewell, Sir Sheriff. Next time you think to cheat someone, remember this feast in Sherwood Forest." Then he slapped the horse on the rump. The horse bolted forward, almost knocking the Sheriff off. The surprised Sheriff had to wave his arms wildly to keep his balance.

"Don't fall, good Sheriff!" Robin called, roaring with laughter as the Sheriff rode away.

The Sheriff didn't only lose his money to Robin that day, but his reputation suffered as well. Men laughed at him, and people even made up songs telling how the Sheriff tried to cheat Robin Hood, only to be cheated himself. Never mess with an honest man like Robin Hood, that's what I always say!

6
Little John Joins the Sheriff

As you know, there are many tales of Robin Hood and the Merry Men. This particular story is about Robin's best friend, Little John. It seems that Little John wanted to have some fun with the Sheriff too....

Spring and summer passed, and the mellow month of October came to the land. The air was cool and fresh, the harvests were gathered from the fields, and the apples were ripe. Even though some months had passed since the Sheriff's feast in Sherwood, he was still angry and embarrassed about the matter and could not bear to hear Robin Hood's name spoken in his presence.

October was also the time for a great fair which was held in Nottingham. People came from far and wide to attend this fair and watch the archery contest that was held there. **And let's not forget about all the food. Mmmm...**

That year, the Sheriff was reluctant to hold the archery contest for fear Robin Hood would attend and make a fool of him again. But he knew that if he canceled the contest, men would laugh and say he was afraid of Robin Hood. So he decided to offer a prize that Robin would not care to win—two fat steers. **Steers are cattle. They need a pasture to graze in, so it would be hard to keep them in a forest.**

When Robin Hood heard what the prize would be, he was angry. "What kind of a prize is the Sheriff offering?" he grumbled. "Only someone with a farm will care to win that. I would have loved nothing better than to have another bout in Nottingham, but two steers will not please or profit me."

"Robin, my friend," said Little John. "Will Stutely and I were at the Sign of the Blue Boar today, and we heard that the Sheriff is offering this prize just so none of us from Sherwood will care to go to the fair. But I would like to try and win those steers anyway, just for Sherwood's good name."

"I would rather you not go," Robin said, "for I don't want anything bad to happen to you. If you must go, then wear a disguise so no one recognizes you. I would hate to lose my friend and right-hand man."

"I will wear a good suit of scarlet instead of this Lincoln green," Little John told him, "and I will cover my head with a broad-brimmed hat. I will even speak with an accent so people will think I am from another place. No one will know me." And so Little John set off to the fair at Nottingham in disguise.

Nottingham was a fine sight that day. Booths and tents covered the grass, with colorful streamers and flower garlands everywhere. In some booths dancing and music could be found. In others food and drink were served, while still others held all manner of things for sale. But the center of attention was a raised platform where two men battled with quarterstaffs.

Little John made his way through the crowd. The tall, strong man dressed in scarlet attracted many stares from the people, but no one recognized Little John from Robin Hood's band.

Little John enjoyed the dancing, the food, and the sports. At last he reached the platform where the quarterstaff matches were being held. Now Little John loved a bout at quarterstaff as much as he loved food and drink, and he decided he would try his hand that day.

When Little John reached the platform, he saw a man named Eric o' Lincoln walking back and forth. Eric had beaten many men that day, and no one else was willing to fight him. He strode up and down, swinging his staff and shouting, "Who will come and strike a blow with me? The blood of Nottingham youth must run slow and cold, for no one has been able to beat this man of Lincoln."

When Eric saw Little John standing head and shoulders above the rest of the crowd, he called, "Hey there, you long-legged fellow in scarlet! Are you brave enough to fight a bout with me, or are you a coward like the other men here?"

"It would please me well to knock some of the boasting out of you!" Little John said. "But I don't have my staff with me this day."

Eric laughed. "Well spoken for one who fears to meet me man to man."

Little John was getting angry. "Is there a man here who will lend me his staff so I may try the mettle of this proud fellow?" he asked. A number of men held their staffs out to him. Little John picked the heaviest one. Then he jumped up on the platform and faced Eric o' Lincoln.

The people at the fair that day saw the greatest bout of quarterstaffs that Nottingham had ever had. At first Eric o' Lincoln had the advantage. Once, twice, thrice Eric struck at Little John, but each time the giant turned the blows away. Then he cracked Eric so soundly that it made the Lincoln man's head ring. "What do you think of that?" John shouted at him. "You don't look so proud of yourself now."

Eric grew furious at Little John's words and his blows. "I'm not finished with you yet!" he said. He began to rain down blows like hail on the roof, but he could not touch Little John. Finally, Little John saw his chance and struck a blow that dropped Eric to the floor.

Everyone shouted with joy as Little John jumped down from the platform in triumph. "I can beat a boastful Lincoln man any day!" Little John cried, grinning. Then he hurried away toward the archery field, for that contest was about to begin.

Many men shot well in the archery contest that day, but of all of them, Little John was the best. The Sheriff had heard how this same tall stranger in scarlet had beaten Eric o' Lincoln at quarterstaffs and won honor for Nottingham that day, and he was anxious to meet him.

"What is your name, good fellow?" the Sheriff asked Little John.

"Men do call me Reynold Greenleaf," Little John replied.

"You are the fairest hand at the longbow that I have ever seen, next to that scoundrel Robin Hood. Will you join my service, good man? I will pay you well."

"I will gladly enter your household," said Little John, for he thought this would be a great joke to play on the Sheriff. "And to show my joy at entering your service, I will give these two fat steers to the good folk here to make a feast."

And so there was much celebrating that night. Meanwhile, Little John headed off to the Sheriff's house, sure he would find some fun and adventure there.

Methinks Little John is walking right into a den of lions by entering the Sheriff's service, but he's not worried at all. Will Little John play a joke on the Sheriff, or will the joke be on him?

7

Little John's Trick

Little John found life in the Sheriff's service to be pretty easy. The Sheriff made Reynold Greenleaf—as he called Little John—his right-hand man and held him in great favor. Soon Little John was sleeping late, eating rich foods, and generally taking it easy. Before he knew it, six months had passed. Then something happened that changed everything.

One morning, the Sheriff and some of his men set off to hunt with some great lords. The Sheriff wanted to show off Reynold Greenleaf's skill to his guests, but he could not find him anywhere, so he had to go off without him.

Where was Little John? He lay in bed snoring until the sun was high in the sky. When he finally woke, he lay still, thinking how fair and beautiful everything was. The sun shone brightly at the window and the air was sweet with spring flowers.

Then, faint and far away, came the sound of a horn. The sound was small but, like a pebble dropped in a fountain, it broke the smooth surface of Little John's thoughts. His spirit seemed to awaken from its sluggishness, and he remembered his happy life in Sherwood Forest. He wondered what his friends were doing now. Were they feasting in the greenwood? Or were they talking about him, wondering when he would return? He knew that someone would have told Robin where he was and what he was doing. Was Robin worried about him? Did he miss his friend?

Little John had entered the Sheriff's service thinking it was a great joke, but now he realized the joke was on him. It seemed that being in the Sheriff's company had changed Little John from a proud, free man to a lazy servant. He had grown so used to his easy life that he had forgotten his friends and his days in the forest.

Little John thought of Robin, his best friend in all the world, and of his other friends, and his heart grew heavy with homesickness. "I will go back to my dear friends," he decided, "and I will not leave them again in this life!" So saying, he leaped from bed, dressed quickly, and headed downstairs.

A pasty is a pie filled with meat and gravy. Delicious!

Little John was hungry, so he headed for the kitchen. In the pantry, he found a great deer pasty, two roasted chickens, and a platter of eggs. "That will do for starters," said Little John.

Just then the cook came running into the kitchen and saw Little John tucking a napkin under his chin.

"Reynold Greenleaf," the cook cried, "what are you doing in my kitchen? You have no right to go in there and eat my food without permission. You are no better than a thief. Come out of there at once."

"Now, cook," said Little John between mouthfuls, "be careful what you ask for! Most times I am a lamb, but if you get between me and my food, I will turn into a raging lion!"

"Come out at once," repeated the cook, drawing his sword, "or you are a coward as well as a thief."

"I warned you," Little John said. "Look out, for now I come forth like a lion!" He hurried out of the pantry with his own sword drawn.

Little John and the cook started toward each other, their swords raised. Suddenly Little John lowered his sword. "It seems a shame to fight with so much good food standing by," he said. "Why, we could have a delicious feast before we fight! What do you say?"

The cook scratched his head, thinking hard. He did love a good meal. "All right, my friend," he said at last. "Let us feast to our heart's content."

So each thrust his sword back into its scabbard and entered the pantry. There they made short work of the food. Neither spoke, for their mouths were too full of hot meat and eggs, but each thought the other was a fine companion.

At last the cook drew a deep breath and sat back, wiping his hands on his napkin. Little John had also had enough. "A good meal always tastes better when it is eaten with a friend," Little John said.

"You are right," the cook agreed. Then he sighed. "I like you as much as if you were my brother, and I wish we did not have to fight," he said. "But it is getting late, and I have my cooking to do before the Sheriff comes home, so let's have our battle now."

Little John agreed. The two drew their swords and fell upon each other as if they would tear each other limb from limb. Their swords clashed together, and sparks flew up in showers. But though they fought for an hour or more, neither could get the better of the other.

"Stop!" Little John shouted at last. "You are the best swordsman I have ever seen. I truly thought I would have beaten you by now."

"I thought the same of you," the cook said, panting.

"It seems to me that rather than try to cut each other's throats, we should be companions instead," Little John said. "Will you go with me to Sherwood Forest and join Robin Hood's band?"

"You are a man after my own heart!" the cook exclaimed. "I will go with you gladly."

They shook hands and prepared to go. Then Little John said, "Why don't we carry off some of the Sheriff's silver plate to give to Robin Hood as a gift?"

During this period, rich men had dishes made of real silver, and sometimes even gold. You'd never catch those guys eating off of paper plates!

So the men took as much silver as they could lay their hands on, stuffed it all in a sack, and headed into Sherwood Forest.

Plunging into the woods, they came at last to the greenwood tree and found Robin Hood and some of his men resting beneath its branches. When Robin saw Little John, he leaped to his feet. "Welcome back!" he said, clapping the big man on the back. "I was afraid you'd like the Sheriff's company so much that I would never see you again in this life. Don't ever leave us for so long again!"

"It's so good to be back," said Little John, grinning. "Look, Robin, I've brought you some gifts from the Sheriff—his cook and his silver plate!"

Robin Hood frowned. "I am glad to have you back, and I welcome your new companion too, but I like it not that you stole the Sheriff's silver like some petty thief. It is not right."

"If you think the Sheriff wouldn't like us to have the plate," said Little John, "I will go and fetch him, so he may tell us so himself." He ran out of the clearing before Robin could call him back.

Little John ran back toward the Sheriff's castle. He'd traveled about five miles when he heard the sounds of men in the forest and found the Sheriff and his friends hunting.

"Reynold Greenleaf, where have you been?" the Sheriff asked him.

"I have been in the forest," Little John answered, "and there I saw an amazing sight. There was a young deer all in green, and about him was a herd of deer, all dressed in green too."

The Sheriff frowned. "Are you dreaming, that you bring me such a wild tale?" he asked.

"No," Little John answered. "Come with me, and I will show you."

Little John led the Sheriff deeper into the forest. "Here we are," Little John said, leading the Sheriff into the clearing where Robin Hood and his men were waiting. "Here are the deer I spoke of."

At this the Sheriff said bitterly, "I thought I remembered your face, but now I know you for sure. You are Little John, and you have betrayed me this day."

Robin Hood stepped forward and said, "Welcome, Sir Sheriff. Have you come to feast with us again today? I am sure you will like our food, for there stands your very own cook!"

Robin led the Sheriff to the seat beneath the greenwood tree and asked one of the Merry Men to bring him food and drink. But the Sheriff could not touch a drop when he saw that it was served on his own silver plate. "These are my own fine dishes you are using!" he shouted. He glared at Little John. "First you steal my cook, and then you steal my plates? How dare you!"

Robin Hood looked at the Sheriff and said, "Last time you came to Sherwood Forest, you were seeking to cheat me and ended up cheating your own self. This time you come seeking no harm, so I will not harm you. Take your silver back again and go home." He led the Sheriff out of the forest and left him standing, bewildered, the sack of silver in his hand.

What a guy! Robin could have kept the Sheriff's silver, but he knew that wasn't the right thing to do. Little John learned an important lesson that day, and he was glad to be back with Robin and his friends.

8
Will Scarlet

One day, not long after Little John came back to the Merry Men, Robin Hood realized that everyone's clothes were looking shabby and torn. He decided it was time to get some new Lincoln green cloth, so he took Little John and another member of the band, Arthur a Bland, and set off to the town of Ancaster to get new clothes for his men. Little did Robin know that he was about to meet a very interesting person along the way!

Robin Hood and his companions walked swiftly along the sunny road to Ancaster. The day was warm and the road was dusty. After they had traveled some distance, Robin grew thirsty. When he saw a spring of cold water bubbling beside the road, he and his men hurried over to get a drink.

After they had cupped their hands and drunk from the spring, Robin and his men rested for a moment by the side of the road. Suddenly Robin pointed down the road and said, "There is a brightly feathered bird!"

The others looked and saw a young man trudging down the highway. His clothes were bright indeed, for he was dressed in scarlet silk from the hat on his head to the shoes on his feet. A fine sword hung from a leather scabbard decorated with golden thread.

"He is dressed too prettily for my taste," said Arthur a Bland. "But his shoulders are broad and he carries himself like a fighter."

"You are right," agreed Little John. "I don't think this lad is the dainty creature he would like people to think he is."

Robin Hood shook his head. "I don't know," he said. "I'll bet if a mouse ran across his path, the boy would faint dead away. I wonder who he is."

Robin stood up and greeted the youth. "Good day, my pretty lad. Are you strong enough to fight with me, or are you afraid to get your fine clothes dirty?"

The young man stood up tall and straight. "I am afraid of no man," he said. "What sort of fight would you like?"

"How about quarterstaffs?" Robin suggested. "There are some fine oak trees there which we could use for staffs."

The youth nodded. Without a word, he hurried to the side of the road and pulled a young oak tree up by the roots. He came back, calmly trimming away the branches as if pulling a tree from the ground were something he did every day.

Little John and Arthur a Bland watched in

wonder. "Did you see that?" Little John whispered to Arthur. "I think our friend Robin will have a rough time with this fellow. He pulled up that tree as if it were a piece of straw!"

Whatever Robin Hood thought of all this, he did not say. He only stepped forward and faced the man. The fight began.

Robin Hood fought well, but so did the stranger. The dust of the highway rose around them like a cloud so that Little John and Arthur could see nothing—they could only hear the staffs banging together. Three times Robin Hood struck the stranger, but the youth did not even stumble.

Finally the young man struck Robin's staff once, twice, three times. Robin staggered under the blows and fell to the ground.

"Stop!" Robin shouted as the stranger stepped forward to hit him again. "I yield to you!"

Little John and Arthur ran forward, but the stranger was not afraid. "If there are two more of you to fight, then fight you I will," he vowed.

"No, we will fight no more," Robin said. He got to his feet, panting and rubbing his sore bones. "What is your name, lad?"

"Gamwell," the youth replied.

"Gamwell!" Robin cried in surprise. "I have family by that name. Where do you come from?"

"From Maxfield Town," answered the stranger. "I am on my way to seek my mother's brother, whom men call Robin Hood. If you could give me directions—"

"Will Gamwell!" Robin shouted, placing his hands on the young man's shoulders. "Don't you know me, lad?"

Will Gamwell stared at Robin in surprise. "I do believe you are my own Uncle Robin," he said. Then each flung their arms around the other and greeted one another warmly.

"I remember when you were just a boy," Robin

said. He had always been fond of his young nephew. "Do you recall how I taught you to shoot an arrow?"

"Yes," Will replied. "I swear, if I had known it was you, I never would have dared lift my hand against you today. I hope I did not hurt you."

"No, no," Robin said, glancing sideways at Little John, who was trying not to laugh. "Never mind all that. Tell me why you have left your father and mother."

"My father's steward was always a rude man," Will began. "He treated my father with great disrespect. It saddened me to hear him speak so boldly to my father, who was ever a patient man and slow to anger. One day, the steward said such mean things to my father that I could stand it no longer and gave him a smack on the ear. Would you believe the fellow died because of it? So my family sent me off to seek you and escape the law."

"For someone who has killed a man and is running from the law, you seem very calm," Robin commented. "But I am very glad to see you, Will, for I have missed you and the fun we had together. You must change your name, for there are sure to be warrants out for your arrest. Since your clothes are so brightly colored, we will call you Will Scarlet."

And so Robin Hood welcomed a new member into his band. Robin decided that he'd had enough adventure for one day, and that they would run their errand in Ancaster some other day. So the four men set off toward Sherwood Forest and home.

Robin is ready to go home after the rough day he's had, but there is another adventure waiting for him on the road to Sherwood. Keep reading to find out what happens next!

Helllooo! Start flipping the book pages and check out the action . . . . Woo-cha!

9
A Mighty Miller

After they had met Will Scarlet and invited him to join the band, Robin Hood and his friends strolled along the road to Sherwood. As they walked, they took turns singing to pass the time. Will Scarlet sang a pretty ballad about true love, and Arthur a Bland followed with a tale from King Arthur's time.

Little John was singing a merry country song when Robin suddenly interrupted him. "Who is that fellow coming along the road?" he asked.

"I don't know," Little John said grumpily, "but I do know it is an ill thing to stop a good song."

"Don't be angry, Little John," Robin said. "I have been watching this man come along, carrying a huge bag over his shoulder, since you began your song, and I am curious to know who he is."

A miller is a man who grinds flour so people can use it to make bread.

Little John peered up the road. "I have seen the man before," he said. "I think he is a miller from beyond Nottingham."

"You're right," Robin said. "I saw him defeat Ned o' Bradford in a quarterstaff bout two weeks ago, and never have I seen a finer piece of fighting."

By this time the young miller had come so near that they could see him clearly. His clothes were dusted with flour and he carried a large sack of meal over his bent back. Tied across the top of the sack was a thick quarterstaff. The young man was well-muscled and strong, and he strode along the road as easily as if his sack were filled with feathers.

"Let us have a joke with this fellow," Robin said. "We will set upon him as if we were common thieves and pretend to rob him. Then we will take him into the forest and give him a feast such as he has never eaten before. What say you, fellows?"

Everyone agreed Robin's idea was a good one. As the miller came opposite to where Robin and his men lay hidden, they jumped out of the bushes and surrounded him.

"Stop!" Robin commanded.

The miller turned slowly and looked at each man in turn. "Who are you?" he asked in a voice like the growl of a great dog.

"We are four good men who would help you carry your heavy load," Robin replied.

"I can carry this sack myself, thank you."

"You mistake my meaning," Robin said. "I mean you might have some heavy coins in your purse that we can lift from you."

The miller backed up in alarm. "I tell you, I

haven't so much as a penny on me. You should know you are on Robin Hood's land. If he finds you trying to rob an honest tradesman like myself, he will clip your ears and chase you all the way to Nottingham."

"I fear Robin Hood no more than I fear myself," Robin declared. "Now give me your money or I will rattle this staff about your head."

"Search me if you like," the miller said bravely, "but you will find nothing in my pockets or my purse."

"Then you have hidden your money at the bottom of that fat sack of meal," Robin said. "Arthur, dump the meal upon the road and see what you find."

"No!" cried the miller. "Don't spoil my good meal. I will give up the money at the bottom of the bag."

Robin nudged Will Scarlet. "Didn't I say there was money hidden there? I have a wondrous nose for gold and silver, do I not?"

The miller untied the top of the bag and thrust his hands deep into the meal. Robin and his men gathered around him, bending forward to see what the miller would bring forth. But while he pretended to be searching for the money, the miller gathered two great handfuls of meal. "Here it is!" he cried, and flung the meal into their faces.

Robin's eyes, nose, and mouth were filled with flour, and so were those of his men. They stumbled backward, blinded and choking. Then the miller

snatched up his staff and began swinging it wildly. Robin and his men couldn't see to defend themselves or even run away. *Thwack! Thwack!* went the miller's staff across their backs. With each blow, great clouds of flour rose from their jackets and drifted in the breeze like smoke.

"Stop!" yelled Robin at last. "I am Robin Hood!"

"You lie!" said the miller, whacking him on the ribs and sending up another cloud of flour. "Good Robin never robbed an honest man!"

Robin fumbled for his horn and blew three loud blasts upon it, calling for help. It happened that Will Stutely and others of the Merry Men were in the forest nearby, and they hurried to their friend's aid. But when they saw Robin and the other men stumbling around, covered from head to toe with white flour, they all burst out laughing.

"What is wrong here, Robin?" Will Stutely asked when he was finally able to talk.

"Can't you see?" Robin shouted. "This fellow has come as near to killing me as any man in the world."

Will Stutely and his men rushed forward and held the miller fast. Robin rubbed the flour out of his eyes and went to stand before his captive, who was now trembling with fear. He glared at the miller angrily, but his temper soon softened. In fact, the situation was so ridiculous that Robin began to roar with laughter, and so did all his men.

"What is your name, good fellow?" Robin asked when he could speak at last.

"Midge the Miller," came the nervous reply.

"You are the mightiest Midge I have ever seen," Robin said, clapping the miller on the shoulder. "I did not really mean to rob you this day, only to play a trick on you, then invite you to a great feast in Sherwood. Now I think the joke was on me!" **A midge is a tiny insect. Robin is making a pun, saying that this Midge is not tiny at all, but a very powerful fellow.**

Midge laughed in relief and finally relaxed.

"Will you leave your dusty mill and join my band?" Robin asked. "You are too brave a fighter to spend your days grinding flour."

"If you can forgive me for the blows I struck when I did not know who you were, then, yes, I will join you," Midge replied. "I have heard many stories about Robin Hood and his generosity and bravery. In fact," Midge added, looking slightly embarrassed, "I have often thought of joining you and your band."

"I forgive you indeed, and I'm proud to have you as a friend," Robin said. "Now, let all of us go back to Sherwood and have a great feast to welcome our new members. I am bruised and sore, but I feel well enough to celebrate!" So saying, Robin led the way into the forest. His men followed him until all were lost from sight.

Robin thought he'd have some fun at the expense of the miller, but instead, it was Midge who had the last laugh! Still, everything came out all right in the end, and Midge the Miller became the newest Merry Man. There are more tales of Robin to be told—all you have to do is turn the page.

10
A Surprise in the Forest

Robin Hood had been in Sherwood Forest for over a year, and he had become quite a hero to the common folk. More and more peasants left their harsh masters to join Robin in the woods. Soon Robin's band grew to over fifty-five men. Personally, I think he could have used a trusty dog or two!

Robin and his men all vowed to harm no poor man or honest knight, to honor all women, and to help the poor any way they could. When Robin first entered Sherwood Forest, he found it filled with bands of robbers and outlaws. These men cared only for themselves, and they would rob poor peasants of their last pennies. Robin soon cleared the woods of these evil men and claimed all of Sherwood Forest as his own. No honest traveler had anything to fear there.

Now Robin had no love for priests or friars, because in those days, many of them oppressed the poor as badly as the rich lords did. Then one day he heard a story about a very different sort of friar, and he knew he had to meet this man at once.

One afternoon, when a light rain fell gently through the trees of Sherwood, Robin and his men were gathered under the great oak tree, listening to the tale of Nicholas, the newest member of the Merry Men.

"I was a blacksmith for the monks at Newstead Abbey," Nicholas told them. "Then I fell ill and could not work, so my lord's soldiers threw me and my old mother out of our house and gave my job to another man. The shock of it all killed my mother."

"That is truly an evil deed," Robin said. "But what else can you expect of monks? Their hearts are made of stone."

"That is true of most of them," Nicholas agreed, "but there is one friar that truly is a good and honest man. His name is Friar Tuck, and he often came to help the poor and sick of my village. Tuck is an enormous man, and he can fight with the longbow or the staff or the sword. He also has a pack of huge dogs that will do anything for him. Friar Tuck is fierce as a lion to anyone who would harm a poor man or woman, but to all others he is humble and kind."

What did I tell you? Dogs make great heroes too!

"I would like to meet this friar," said Robin, "for he is a man after my own heart."

Several days later, Robin took some of his men and headed into the forest, in search of the mysterious friar.

Robin and his men traveled for many hours.

Finally they came to a low house beside a stream. Robin spied a path winding through the trees nearby, and there he saw a man sitting quietly, dressed in the rough habit of a monk. Even at a distance, Robin could see the man was big and broad, with arms as thick and strong as tree trunks.

"That must be Friar Tuck. He is certainly a sturdy friar!" Robin said. "Let me test him and see what sort of man he is. You men hide yourselves in the trees and don't come out unless I call you."

Robin stepped up to the friar and said, "Hello there, holy man. I have business on the other side of the stream, and I don't care to get my feet wet. Carry me across on your broad back."

Friar Tuck stared at Robin for a moment, as if he didn't understand what Robin was talking about. Then he got up slowly and bent his back so Robin could climb on. The friar walked into the stream and waded across. When he reached the other side, he stepped up onto the bank, and Robin prepared to leap off.

Suddenly Robin felt his left leg seized in an iron grip, while the friar thumped him hard on the ribs. Then Friar Tuck swung Robin around and dumped him into the water.

Robin jumped to his feet, spitting out water and shaking the wet hair out of his eyes. "Now, my fine fellow, carry me back to the place where I was resting or you shall suffer for it," the friar said.

Robin was angry at having his own trick turned against him. He tried to grab his sword, but Friar Tuck

caught his wrist and held it firm. "Carry me back," the friar repeated, smiling.

Robin was surprised that Friar Tuck did not hurt him even though he had the chance. He knew most other men would have given him a sound beating if they were in the friar's place. Without a word, he bent his back and carried the friar back across the stream. But when Robin reached the other side, he whirled around and sent the friar splashing into the water.

"Why you—" Friar Tuck sputtered. Then he looked at Robin, who was still dripping from his dunking in the stream, and burst out laughing.

Robin could not help laughing himself. "Don't we make a pretty sight," he said. He gave the friar his hand, and the two dragged themselves up onto the bank.

Just then, Robin saw a slim youth running toward them, a hood over his head and a bow slung over his back. When the youth raised his hood, Robin got the shock of his life.

"Marian?" he cried, for it was his own true love standing there. "What are you doing here?"

"Don't be angry with me, Robin," she said, hurrying forward to kiss him. "I have been so afraid for you that I came to the forest seeking news of you. I have been spending a great deal of time in the woods lately, learning how to find food and survive in the wild. You remember how we shot arrows and hunted when we were children together in Locksley? Why shouldn't I do that with you now?"

"Because I am an outlaw, sweetheart, and you are a lord's daughter," Robin told her. "Anyone who runs with me is always in danger." Despite his words, Robin stepped forward and hugged Marian tightly. "I have missed you so much. But tell me, how do you know this rascal friar?"

"He is no rascal, Robin, but a good man," answered Marian. "He is a good friend of my uncle, Sir Richard of the Lea, and he holds you in high regard. When I came to the greenwood to learn more about your life, Friar Tuck helped me."

Just then, the friar stepped forward to join them. Robin held out his hand to him. "I hear you have been a true friend to the lady I love," Robin said. "I would like you to be my friend also."

"Robin," replied Friar Tuck with a smile, "I have wished you well since I first heard about you. I think we are not enemies at heart, lad." He gave Robin's hand a squeeze that would have crushed a weaker man's bones, but Robin's grip was almost as strong.

Then the friar turned to smile at Marian. "Robin, you must be a proud man to hold the love of such a fine maiden," he said.

"I am proud," Robin said, "and yet I am sad too. I want more than anything to have Marian with me, for I love her very much. But I am an outlaw. What kind of life can I offer her? Instead of fine things, she would have only the hard life of the wild forest, and she would always be in danger. As much as I want her with me, I cannot risk her life and ask her to be my wife."

"Robin," said Marian, linking her fingers through Robin's, "I love you, and I will marry no other man. I love the woodland life as much as you do, and I am happy here. You think I will change my mind when the cold winds of winter blow. But I know my heart would be warm having you to turn to."

There were tears in Marian's eyes. Robin lifted her hands to his face and kissed them. "I know you love me, but you deserve to be well taken care of. That is the life I wish for you, even though it means we must be apart. But I promise you this—if ever you are in danger, send for me and I will come. And if the day comes when you are no longer safe outside Sherwood Forest, we shall be married by this good friar here and face whatever the future holds together."

Marian and Robin visited with Friar Tuck for some time. As the day grew late, Robin escorted Marian back home. They parted sweetly, knowing that even though they could not be together right then, their love would always last.

How romantic! Marian is truly the girl for Robin, even though they can't be together just yet. No one knows what the future holds, but I'll bet it will be filled with more adventure!

11

The Sorrowful Knight

Robin and his men often went looking for guests to bring to their camp. Poor people were given a fine feast there, and left with gifts of food and money to help them. Rich people also enjoyed a fine meal, but they were asked to leave behind money or goods to pay for the band's hospitality. Robin would then give these gifts to the poor.

You might think Robin worried that the rich men he brought to his camp might return with an army to capture Robin and his friends. But Robin Hood's camp was hidden so deeply in the forest that no one could find it on their own. So Robin continued to bring both rich and poor to sample his band's hospitality.

Spring passed, and summer too, until the golden days of autumn lay upon the land. One fine day, Robin Hood said to Little John, "Today is too fine a day to waste. Take some men and travel toward the east, while I travel toward the west with other members of the band. Each of us shall bring back a guest to dine with us today under the greenwood tree."

Little John agreed. And so they set off in opposite directions to see whom they might meet.

Robin and his companions walked many a mile that day, but they met no likely guests along the road. They stopped at noon to eat a meal behind the tall hedges that grew along the road. As they lay resting on the grass, Robin spied a knight riding slowly toward them.

This knight was the saddest man Robin had ever seen. His head was bowed and his hands hung limply at his sides. Even his horse walked with his head hanging, as if he shared his master's grief.

"Wait here while I look into this matter," Robin told his men and stepped out into the road. "Stop, Sir Knight," Robin said as the man rode up to him. "I have a few words to say to you."

"Who are you who stops a traveler this way?" asked the knight.

"That is a hard question," Robin said. "One man calls me kind, while another calls me cruel. One calls me a good, honest fellow, while another calls me a thief. My name is Robin Hood."

"Robin Hood!" the knight said, a smile crossing his stern face. "I have heard many good things about you. You are the beloved of my niece, Maid Marian."

"Sir Richard of the Lea!" Robin cried in surprise, for this was indeed his true love's uncle. "I did not recognize you. Come and dine with me this day in Sherwood Forest, and I will give you as wonderful a feast as you have ever had in your life."

"You are kind," said Sir Richard, "but I'm afraid you will find me a sorrowful guest."

"I always try to help those who walk in sorrow," Robin told him. "Come, Sir Richard, cheer up and come with us into the forest. Perhaps I can help you with your troubles."

"I doubt that," Sir Richard said, "but I will go with you."

Sir Richard turned his horse toward Sherwood and headed in that direction with Robin and his men walking at his side. After they had walked for a while, Robin asked, "Can you tell me what is making you so unhappy?"

"My castle and my lands are being held against a debt of four hundred pounds which I owe to the Prior of Emmet. The money must be paid in three days, or all I own will belong to the prior." **A prior is a man in charge of a religious community. These men were very rich and powerful in Robin Hood's day.**

"Don't you have the money to pay your debt?" Robin asked.

"No. My son killed a man in a joust. The death was an accident, but this man had powerful friends, and they threatened to have my son arrested. To save him from prison, I had to pay a huge ransom. All my money went to save my son, and now I cannot save myself." **Jousts were popular entertainment. They were contests where two knights battled each other on horseback. Very exciting!**

"Have you no friends to help you?" asked Will Scarlet.

Sir Richard shook his head. "I had many friends when I was rich. Now that I am poor, my friends have left me, and all I have are enemies."

"Many have found Robin Hood a friend in their troubles," Robin said. "Cheer up, Sir Knight. I may be able to help you yet."

Evening was coming on by the time the group reached the greenwood tree. Little John was already there with his guest. Robin was pleased to see that this guest was none other than the Bishop of Hereford, one of the most powerful men in the land. He was also one of the richest. Even though he was a man of the Church, the bishop thought nothing of taking money from the poor. He was no better than Robin's old enemy, the Sheriff of Nottingham.

The bishop did not look happy to be in Sherwood Forest this day. He paced back and forth like a fox caught in a trap. Tied to a nearby tree were several horses, each loaded down with packs and boxes. Robin's eyes gleamed at the sight.

"How dare your men treat me this way!" the bishop shouted when he saw Robin. "How dare they stop me, an important man of the Church, and bring me here, making jokes about me all the way. I have never been so insulted in all my life! I even found a false priest dwelling here," he said, pointing at Friar Tuck. "What a disgrace!"

"I am as holy a man as you are," Friar Tuck said.

"Don't be insulted by our teasing, Lord Bishop," Robin told him. "Not a man here would harm you.

Now, sit down and enjoy yourself while we prepare a feast for you. See, here is another guest to join you at the feast." Robin bade Sir Richard sit beside the bishop.

Before long, the feast was spread before them. Torches were lit to brighten the clearing, and all the men enjoyed the delicious food spread over the grass. When everyone had eaten his fill, Robin Hood called for silence.

"I have a story to tell all of you," Robin said, and he related the sad tale of Sir Richard and his debts. When he had finished, he turned to the bishop. "Don't you think it is a terrible thing for a man of the Church to take a poor knight's lands from him?"

The bishop did not answer. "You are the richest bishop in all of England," Robin went on. "Won't you help this needy man?" Still the bishop said nothing.

"Little John, you and Will Stutely fetch the packs from the bishop's horses," Robin ordered. The men did as they were told. Among the goods, Robin found a paper listing who the items were meant for. He gave the paper to Will Scarlet to read aloud.

"'Three bales of silk to Quentin of Ancaster,'" Will read.

"We shall not touch that," said Robin, "for Quentin is an honest fellow."

"'One bale of velvet for the Abbey of Beaumont,'" Will continued.

"What do those priests need with velvet?" Robin asked. "Well, I will not take it all from them. Measure it into three lots—one to be sold for charity, one for us, and one for the abbey."

So the list was gone through, and the goods were judged as Robin saw fit. At last they came to the final item.

"'A treasure box belonging to the Bishop of Hereford,'" Will read from the list.

As the bishop watched, trembling, Robin's men opened the box. A great pile of gold rolled out, gleaming in the torchlight. When the money was all counted, it came to fifteen hundred pounds.

"My Lord Bishop," said Robin, "I will not strip you as clean as a winter's hedge. You shall take back one third of your money—five hundred pounds. One third you can well spare to pay us for your feast, for you are a rich man. The last third will go to help some needy soul."

Robin turned to Sir Richard and said, "Since it is a man of the Church who seeks to ruin you, the Church's money shall be used to save you. Take this five hundred pounds and pay your debt to the prior with it."

Sir Richard stared at Robin and tears filled his eyes. At last he said, "I thank you from the bottom of my heart. I will take the money and pay my debts, but I solemnly promise that in a year and a day, I will pay you back the full amount." Robin agreed, for he knew Sir Richard would be true to his word and pay back his debt.

So the money was divided up, and Sir Richard's

share was placed in a leather bag and given to him. "Now I must get home," the knight said, "for my lady wife will be worried about me."

"Let me and some of the other men lead Sir Richard safely out of the forest," Little John suggested. Robin quickly agreed.

Then Will Stutely said, "Let us give Sir Richard our bale of velvet as a present for his lady wife."

"You have spoken well, and it shall be done," Robin said.

"My good friends," said the knight, "Sir Richard of the Lea will always remember your kindness. If ever you should be in trouble, come to me. The walls of Castle Lea shall fall before any harm can come to you." He shook Robin's hand to seal his promise, and a joyful shout went up from all of the men.

Robin made the Bishop of Hereford stay with him for three days, in case he thought to stop Sir Richard from paying his debts. Although Robin and his men held many sporting contests to amuse the bishop and fed him with the finest foods, the bishop was angry and humiliated at being Robin's guest. When he finally left, he promised himself that he would someday make Robin Hood regret all that had happened at that feast in Sherwood Forest.

Robin Hood has really done a good deed this day! He has a good friend in Sir Richard—and he's going to need a friend in the days to come.

12
Robin Meets the Queen

One day the following summer, a strange sight was seen on the road to Sherwood Forest. A young man rode along on a beautiful white horse. This fellow was a handsome sight, for he was dressed in the finest silk and velvet, and his long yellow hair flowed out behind him as he rode. This was Richard Partington, page to Her Majesty, Queen Eleanor.

The road was hot and dusty, so young Richard was glad when he saw the Blue Boar Inn on the side of the road. The boy stopped his horse and called for a cool drink to be brought outside.

A page is a boy in training to become a knight.

Little John and several of the Merry Men were seated in the shade under a tree in front of the tavern. When Richard received his drink, he raised the glass and said to them, "Here's to my royal mistress, noble Queen Eleanor. May my journey soon have an end, for in her name I seek the man called Robin Hood."

"Why does the Queen seek Robin Hood?" Little John asked. "Does she wish to harm him?"

"No," the page replied. "She has heard many fine stories of his skill at archery. She wishes to invite Robin to compete in a great archery contest at Finsbury Fields."

Little John and his friends decided it would be safe to bring Richard Partington into Sherwood, so they led him to the greenwood tree and introduced him to Robin Hood.

Richard gave Robin a beautiful ring. "This ring comes from Her Royal Highness, Queen Eleanor. She wishes you to come to London to compete in a great archery contest there, so she can see for herself your great skill with a bow and arrow."

Robin kissed the ring and slipped it onto his finger. "Sooner would I lose my life than this ring," he said. "I will do as the Queen asks and go with you to London."

"The Queen also says that you may take any members of your band with you and she will welcome them," Richard went on.

Robin chose Little John, Will Scarlet, and his minstrel, Allan a Dale, to journey to London with him. He also put Will Stutely in charge of the band while he was away. The travelers quickly dressed in their finest clothes and set off behind Richard on the road to London.

In five days' time, Robin and his companions reached the walls of famous London Town. They hurried to the castle and were taken into Queen Eleanor's own room to meet her.

Robin and his men knelt before the Queen. "Here am I, Robin Hood," he said. "I came at your request, for I am your loyal servant and would do anything you ask."

The Queen smiled and motioned the men to their feet. Then she ordered food and drink to be brought while they rested from their long journey.

After they had eaten their fill, Queen Eleanor asked all about their adventures in Sherwood Forest. She and her ladies-in-waiting all laughed at the exciting tales, and so the time passed until it was time for the great archery contest at Finsbury Fields.

Finsbury Fields was a fine sight the morning of the contest. The field was ringed with the bright banners and flags of the archers from the King's guard who were going to compete. Seats had been set up for the crowd on either side, and there was a raised platform for the King and Queen, hung all around with colorful streamers. The targets were lined up on the far end of the field, and everything was ready for the arrival of the King and Queen.

At last, six trumpeters rode into the clearing, blowing a fanfare on their horns. Behind them came King Henry upon a fine gray horse. Queen Eleanor rode beside him on a beautiful white mare. Their men-at-arms marched beside them, and behind them came all the members of the court, filling the lawn with bright colors.

Everyone shouted with joy as the King and

Queen took their seats on the platform. Then the archers came marching onto the field and stood before the King. His heart swelled with pride at the sight of his fine men.

The King's herald announced the rules and the prizes. The best archer would win thirty pounds in gold and ten fine arrows. The second prize was a herd of fat deer from the King's own lands, and the third was a cask of fine wine. When they heard of these prizes, the archers raised their bows in the air and shouted their approval.

The contest began. Now Queen Eleanor loved to tease her husband, King Henry, and she also loved a good joke. Today she had it in her mind to play a prank on her husband, the King. That was why she had invited Robin and his men to London.

As they watched the fine shooting, the Queen asked the King, "Do you think these men are the finest archers in the land?"

"Indeed I do," the King replied. "I would say they are the finest archers in all the world."

"What would you say if I could find three archers to match the best men here?"

"I would say that is impossible," the King replied. "No one can match the shooting of my guard."

"I will make a wager with you," said Queen Eleanor, "that I can find three sturdy men to match any three of your guards this very day. All I ask is that you grant a pardon to anyone who comes on my behalf."

The King laughed when he heard this. "All right," he agreed, "I will grant these men a pardon for forty days, to come and go as they please. Not only that, but if these men can beat my archers, I will give them the prizes from today's contest."

"So be it," said the Queen. She motioned to young Richard Partington and whispered in his ear. The young man bowed and hurried away, disappearing into the crowd.

At last the contest ended. The three top archers were named Gilbert, Tepus, and Hubert, and the King knew all of them well. As they stood before the King, Richard Partington rushed across the field, followed by three strangers carrying bows and arrows. The strangers bowed before King Henry and Queen Eleanor. King Henry peered at them closely, but he did not recognize them. The Bishop of Hereford, however, was sitting close beside the King. When he saw the three archers, he jumped as though stung by a wasp.

The Queen leaned forward toward the men. "Now Locksley," she said to Robin Hood, "I have laid a wager with the King that you and your men can outshoot anyone he sends against you. Will you do your best for my sake?"

"Yes," said Robin. "I will do my best this day or never shoot an arrow again."

"Who are these men?" King Henry asked the Queen.

Queen Eleanor was about to speak, but the bishop could hold his tongue no longer. "They are a

band of outlaws from Nottingham," he said. "Their names are Robin Hood, Little John, and Will Scarlet."

At this, the King frowned. "Is this true?" he asked the Queen.

Queen Eleanor smiled. "Yes," she said, "the

bishop has told the truth. He should know these men well, for he once feasted with them in Sherwood Forest. But remember, you promised not to harm these men for forty days."

"I will keep my promise," King Henry said angrily. "But when the forty days are over, this outlaw had better be careful." He turned to Gilbert, Tepus, and Hubert. "I have pledged that you three will shoot against these men," he told them. "If you outshoot them, I will fill your caps with silver pennies. If you lose, I will take your prizes away and give them to Robin Hood and his men. Do your best and win this bout for me!"

News of this strange new contest spread quickly through the crowd. Soon everyone was buzzing with the news that Robin Hood himself was to shoot against the King's men.

Six fresh targets were set up and each man was given three chances. Hubert of Suffolk was the first to shoot. His arrows all lodged near the center of the target, and the crowd shouted their approval.

Will Scarlet was next, but he was nervous, and the first arrow he shot missed the center completely. "Take care!" said Robin, and Will's next two shots lodged squarely in the center ring. But Hubert had done better this day.

"If your archers shoot no better than that, you are likely to lose your wager," King Henry said to Queen Eleanor. But she only smiled, for she knew she could count on Robin Hood and Little John.

Tepus was next. He too was nervous, and only two of his shots struck the center ring. Little John had no trouble beating him, for all three of the big man's arrows landed in the center.

Gilbert was the next to shoot. He had taken first prize in the King's contest, and his luck continued to be good. Three arrows he shot, and three arrows he landed in the center.

"Well done, Gilbert!" said Robin Hood, clapping him on the shoulder. "You should join me in the greenwood, for you are too good an archer to be trapped behind the gray walls of London Town." Some members of the crowd heard what Robin said and murmured in surprise at his boldness. Gilbert only shrugged and smiled.

Robin took his place and picked three fine shafts from his quiver of arrows. "Indeed," Robin continued as he drew his bow, "in London, you can find nothing to shoot at but ravens and crows." He loosed his arrow, and it flew into the center of the target. "In Sherwood, you can tickle the ribs of the finest deer in England." Laughing, he loosed his second arrow. This one also lodged in the center, just to the left of the first. Without pausing, Robin let fly his third arrow. It dropped between the other two arrows, in the very center of the ring.

A low murmur ran through the crowd, for never had London seen such fine shooting. Gilbert shook Robin's hand and admitted he had been beaten.

"I can't believe two of my finest archers have

been beaten by a couple of outlaws," King Henry said under his breath. "I have never been so humiliated in all my life!" Glaring at the Queen, he got to his feet and stomped off the field.

Robin and his men were surrounded by a great crowd of people. Everyone wanted to meet and talk to these famous outlaws and wonderful archers. Then one of the King's guard pushed his way through the crowd and tugged at Robin's sleeve. "I bring you a message from Richard Partington. He said that a certain lady tells you, 'The lion growls. Beware.'"

Robin knew it was Queen Eleanor who had sent the message, and that she was warning him to beware of the King's anger. He called his men together, and they left London as fast as they could.

Queen Eleanor may have won her wager, but there isn't much she can do to stop King Henry if he decides to hurt Robin. I think the King is angry enough to do just that!

13
Hunted!

It was a good thing Robin and his men left London in such a hurry. They'd barely gone a few miles when six of King Henry's biggest, meanest guards pushed their way through the crowd at Finsbury Fields. They were looking for Robin, and they meant to arrest him!

Wait a minute! Didn't King Henry promise Queen Eleanor that he wouldn't hurt Robin for forty days? Well, yes, but the King was so angry at losing the bet with his wife—and so embarrassed that his men had lost the contest to Robin Hood—that he broke his promise. Robin's old enemy, the Bishop of Hereford, also had something to do with King Henry's actions, because he talked him into going after Robin. The bishop had sworn to get revenge for the time Robin held him in Sherwood Forest, and now was his chance. Robin didn't know it then, but he was in great danger!

Robin Hood, Little John, Will Scarlet, and Allan a Dale walked until twilight covered the land. Then, thinking they were far enough from London, they stopped at a cheery little inn to rest for the night.

Robin and his friends had just finished their

supper when the owner of the inn told him that a young man named Richard Partington was waiting outside and needed to speak with Robin immediately. Robin hurried out to talk to him.

"I heard you had taken this road out of London," Richard told Robin. "I am glad to have caught up with you at last. The Queen has asked me to tell you that King Henry has been turned against you by the Bishop of Hereford. He sent men to arrest you at Finsbury Fields, but you had already left. Now he has gathered an army and is sending them along this road, under the Bishop of Hereford's command. They mean to take you prisoner before you can reach Sherwood. You had best leave this inn right away, or else you will be sleeping in a cold dungeon tonight!"

"This is the second time you have saved my life," Robin said. "If the time ever comes, I will show you that Robin Hood never forgets such good deeds. We will leave this inn tonight, telling the innkeeper that we are headed to St. Albans. That is far from Sherwood, so if the King's men head in that direction, they will not be on our trail. I will go one way and my men will go another. We will travel back to Sherwood by such crooked paths that the King's men will never find us."

Robin hurried back inside and quickly told his men of Richard's message. They left the inn and headed back to Sherwood at once. At Robin's orders, Little John, Will Scarlet, and Allan a Dale traveled back to Sherwood by one path, while Robin took another.

It took Little John and his companions eight days to reach Sherwood Forest. But when they reached the greenwood tree, they found that Robin had not yet returned. What had happened to him?

Robin had traveled for seven days. He saw not one of King Henry's men, and began to think he would reach Sherwood without any trouble. "Surely the bishop and his men are far away in St. Albans, looking for me there!" he said with a laugh. "I have nothing to fear."

The bishop and his army had indeed gone to St. Albans, but when he realized that Robin had once more slipped out of his trap, the bishop stopped not a minute. He gathered his army together and headed toward Nottingham as fast as he could. Then he divided his men into groups and sent them through the countryside to block every road leading toward Sherwood. The Sheriff of Nottingham also joined the hunt. Little John, Will Scarlet, and Allan a Dale had made it back to Sherwood just before the army arrived, but Robin was not so lucky.

Robin had no idea any of this was going on, and he whistled merrily as he headed those last few miles toward Sherwood. He stopped to drink at a little stream when suddenly an arrow whistled past his ear. Quick as a wink, Robin leaped across the stream and plunged into the thick woods beside the road. Six more arrows rattled after him.

Some of King Henry's men came galloping up the road. They leaped from their horses and raced into the trees after Robin, but Robin knew the land better than they did. Crawling, hiding, and running, he finally managed to leave them far behind and find another road to Sherwood.

Robin had not gone far when he saw another group of the King's men camped alongside the road. Robin ran the other way, only to meet yet another army there. They raised a great shout when they saw him, but Robin ran as fast as he could. He didn't stop until he was far from Sherwood.

Finally, an exhausted Robin sat down beneath a hedge to catch his breath. "That was the nearest escape I've ever had in my life!" he said. "All that running has made me hungry and thirsty. If only there was some way I could get a tasty meal."

Just then, Robin spied a cobbler walking down the road. **A cobbler is someone who makes and repairs shoes.** "Hello there," Robin called as the man drew closer. "What is your name, and what do you have in that bag at your side?"

"My name is Quince," the cobbler replied. "I carry a fat hen for roasting. I will have a fine feast this day."

"A fat hen sounds like a tasty treat," Robin said. "Tell me, Quince, would you sell that hen to me? I will give you the colorful clothes I am wearing and ten shillings too, in exchange for your clothes and leather apron and your meal."

"You are joking with me," said Quince. "My clothes are old and patched, and yours are much finer."

"No, I am not joking," Robin said. "I like your clothes very much. Come, let us trade." He stood and took off his jacket. Seeing that he was serious, Quince did the same. Soon each man was wearing the other's clothes.

"Now let us have that feast you spoke of," Robin said. The two men sat down by the side of the road and ate so heartily that soon there was nothing left of that fat hen but bones.

Suddenly six of King Henry's men burst upon them where they sat and pulled Quince roughly to his feet. "We have caught you at last, you outlaw! Don't look so innocent," said one of the guard as Quince looked around in confusion. "We know by your colorful clothes that you are that rascal, Robin Hood!"

"Am I Robin Hood?" replied Quince. "I thought I was Quince the Cobbler."

"Your rough treatment of this man has scrambled his wits," Robin told the soldiers. "I myself am Quince the Cobbler, not this man!"

The soldiers led poor Quince away. After they had gone, Robin chuckled at the joke he had played upon the soldiers. He knew no harm would come to Quince, for as soon as the bishop saw him, he would realize the cobbler was not Robin Hood and set him free.

Robin started out toward Sherwood once more. He thought to travel straight on without stopping, but he had only gone a few miles when he felt sleepiness stealing over him. When he came to an inn, he decided to spend the night there and travel on in the morning.

The inn was very small and had only three bedrooms. The innkeeper, seeing how poorly Robin was dressed, showed him to the smallest room. Robin didn't care, for he was so tired that he would have slept on broken stones. He rolled into bed and was asleep before his head touched the pillow.

Soon after Robin had gone to bed, a terrible thunderstorm came up. The inn began to fill with travelers who needed shelter from the storm. By the time a friar from Emmet Priory arrived at the inn, there was no room left. He had to share the room with Robin.

"Do you really expect me to share a room with a simple cobbler?" the friar said to the innkeeper.

"I'm sorry, sir," said the innkeeper, "but this is the only room we have left."

"I have never been so insulted!" said the proud friar. Just then, a clap of thunder shook the walls of the inn. "Very well," the friar huffed. "I suppose this is better than being outside in this awful storm." He sat down on the other bed, glaring at the innkeeper and at Robin.

Robin and the friar both slept soundly that night. When Robin opened his eyes at dawn, he was surprised to see who was sharing his room. Then he got an idea. "Good friar," he said to the sleeping monk, "you have borrowed my room, so I will borrow your clothes." So Robin put on the friar's gown and left his cobbler's clothes in its place.

As for the friar, he was furious when he woke up

and discovered what Robin had done. But he had no choice—either wear the cobbler's clothes or go without any clothes at all. And so the friar set off down the road, grumbling to himself. He had not gone far when a band of King Henry's soldiers stepped out of the trees and blocked the road in front of him. "At last we have caught you, Robin Hood!" their leader shouted. Two soldiers rushed forward and grabbed the friar's arms.

"Let go of me!" the friar demanded, but his words only made the soldiers hold him tighter. "I am not Robin Hood! I am a simple friar!"

"If you are not Robin Hood, then why are you wearing his clothes?" one of the soldiers asked him.

"My own clothes were stolen!" the friar protested. "I shared a room at the inn with a man, and he—"

"Tell it to the bishop," the soldier interrupted him. "That's who we're taking you to see."

"I tell you, I am not Robin Hood!" the friar shouted, but the soldiers would not believe him. It wasn't until he came before the Bishop of Hereford himself that the friar's true identity was made known. And the bishop realized that Robin Hood had tricked him and escaped his clutches once again.

Meanwhile, Robin traveled along happily in the friar's clothes, passing two bands of the King's men along the way. Then he came upon a knight riding along the road. Robin recognized the man at once.

"Sir Richard!" Robin cried, for it was his old friend, Sir Richard of the Lea. "I am glad to see you." He told Sir Richard of all that had happened to him since King Henry had broken his promise.

Sir Richard shook his head. "You are in great danger, Robin. The woods are full of soldiers—both King Henry's men and the Sheriff's. There is only one thing for you to do. You must go back to London and throw yourself on Queen Eleanor's mercy. Only she can protect you from the King's anger. Come to my castle and change your clothes. Then my men and I will bring you to London." So Robin went with Sir Richard and did what he said, for he knew it was his only chance.

Queen Eleanor was walking in her royal garden with six of her ladies-in-waiting. Suddenly a man jumped over the wall and landed right at the Queen's feet. All the ladies screamed in fear, but Queen Eleanor recognized Robin Hood at once.

"How now, Robin?" she said. "Do you dare come into the very jaws of the lion? Don't you know the King is seeking you all over England?"

"Yes," Robin said. "That is why I have come. I know you are kind and merciful, and I lay my life in your hands."

"I will give you my aid and do all I can to see you back to Sherwood in safety," the Queen promised. "Wait here until I return."

Queen Eleanor found King Henry meeting with his advisers. "My good husband, I have an unbelievable tale to tell you. The outlaw, Robin Hood, who you have been hunting for many a day, has turned up here at this very castle."

"What!" the King shouted in surprise. "I will have my men seize him immediately!"

"Wait!" Queen Eleanor said. "Don't you find it remarkable that a hunted man would come back to the home of his hunter? Surely it takes someone of great courage to do that."

"Yes, but—" King Henry began.

"You have always admired courage," Queen Eleanor reminded her husband. "How can you fail to reward it now?"

"This man is an outlaw, a common criminal!" King Henry shouted. "He beat my men in a contest and made me look like a fool. I owe him no mercy!"

"But I do," the Queen told him. "He has thrown himself on my mercy, and I intend to do all I can to reward his faith in me. Good husband, on the day of the archery contest, you promised you would not harm Robin Hood and his men. The fact that you broke that promise shames me, and it should shame you as well."

King Henry frowned. It did bother him that people might think he was not true to his word.

"For your own honor, and for the love you bear for me," the Queen said, "let Robin Hood return home safely."

The King thought for a long time. Finally, he nodded. "It shall be done," he agreed.

Queen Eleanor hurried back to the garden where Robin was waiting. "The King has agreed to let you go in peace and safety," she told Robin. "He will send his page with you to see that no one arrests you on your journey home. You have me to thank for your good fortune, for without my strong words to the King, you would be a dead man! You have put your head in the angry lion's mouth, yet you escaped by a miracle. Do not be so bold again."

The King was true to his word this time, and Robin was soon safe at home in his beloved Sherwood Forest. So his adventures in London finally came to a happy end.

Whew! That was too close for comfort! It certainly helps to have friends in high places! Robin is safe for now, but if I know him, his life won't remain quiet for long!

14
A Terrible Battle

Several years passed after Robin's adventures in London. These years brought many changes to England. The biggest change was that King Henry died. Now England had a new ruler, King Henry's son Richard. He was called Richard of the Lion's Heart because he was so brave and daring. This King loved nothing better than an adventure, and he was always leading his armies into battle.

Having a new King didn't make much difference in Sherwood Forest. The days continued much as they had before.

Remember the Sheriff of Nottingham? He'd left Robin alone for a while, but he still hated the outlaw as much as ever. Now the Sheriff thought he could win King Richard's favor by trying again to rid Sherwood Forest of Robin Hood. No plan was too evil or sneaky for the Sheriff, and so he came up with a new plot to get rid of Robin Hood once and for all.

It was a fresh, bright summer day in Sherwood Forest. Robin Hood and Little John walked down a forest path, enjoying the warm sunshine.

"I have a feeling something exciting is going to happen today," Robin said.

Little John quickly agreed. "Here are two paths. You take the one on the right, and I will take the one on the left."

"But be careful," Robin said to his friend. "I would not have any harm befall you for all the world."

Little John laughed. "You are more likely to get into danger than I am," he said. The two shook hands and set upon their separate ways.

Robin Hood strolled along the wide woodland path until he came upon a man sitting under the shade of a large oak tree. Robin had never seen anything like this man. From head to toe he was dressed in a horse's hide. The hood over his head still had the horse's ears on it! By his side was a heavy sword. A quiver of arrows hung across his shoulders and a strong bow leaned against the tree.

"Hello, friend," Robin said. "Who are you, and what are you wearing? I have never seen such a strange sight in all my life!"

The strange man did not answer. He pushed the hood back from his head and stared at Robin with hard black eyes like a hawk's. His face was so cruel that it made Robin's flesh crawl.

"Who are you, rascal?" the stranger asked at last in a harsh voice.

"Speak not so sourly. Have you feasted on vinegar today, to make your words so bitter?"

"If you don't like my words, you'd best be going," the stranger growled. "My deeds are just as sour."

Robin just smiled and sat down beside the stranger. The two looked at each other for a long time. Finally, the man asked Robin, "What is your name?"

"Oh, it may be this or it may be that," Robin answered. "I think it is more important for you to tell me your name, since you are a stranger in these parts. And tell me, why are you wearing such strange clothes?"

At these words the other man broke into a harsh roar of laughter. "You are a brave man to speak to me so boldly. I wear these clothes to keep my body warm and to protect myself from swords and arrows. As for my name, it is Guy of Gisbourne. I come from Herefordshire, and I am an outlaw. Not long ago, the Bishop of Hereford summoned me and said that if I did a favor for the Sheriff of Nottingham, the bishop would pardon me and give me two hundred pounds. So I came to Nottingham and found the Sheriff. The favor he wanted was for me to hunt down an outlaw named Robin Hood and take him alive or dead. I agreed to do this, for I would shed the blood of my own brother for two hundred pounds."

Robin listened to all of this with anger growing in his heart. He had heard of this Guy of Gisbourne, and knew him to be the bloodiest outlaw in all of England, for he showed mercy to no man.

What would you expect of a guy wearing a horse's hide? Blech!

"I have heard of you," Robin replied when Guy had finished his story. "I think there is no one Robin Hood would rather meet than you."

At this, Guy gave another harsh laugh. "It will be a sad day for Robin Hood when he meets me," he said.

"What if this Robin Hood is a better fighter than you?" Robin asked.

"I would bet my life that is not true," Guy said. "Some call him a great archer, but I would not be afraid to challenge him."

"Many of us in Nottingham are good with a bow and arrow," Robin said. "Even I would not fear to shoot a round with you."

"I like your spirit," said Guy. "Put up a target and we will see who is the better archer."

So Robin Hood cut a branch about twice the thickness of a man's thumb and set it up a good distance away. "That is the sort of mark that we men of Nottingham shoot at," Robin said. "Let's see you split that wand if you call yourself an archer."

"No one could hit a mark like that!" Guy snarled, but Robin only smiled. So Guy strung his bow. He shot two arrows toward the target, but both missed their mark.

Robin laughed. "If you are no better with a sword than you are with a bow and arrow, you will never overcome Robin Hood," he told the stranger.

"You had better watch what you say to me," Guy growled. His hand moved to his sword, as if he meant to attack Robin for daring to say such a thing to him.

"Let me take my turn now," Robin said calmly. Then he drew his own bow.

Robin's first arrow passed within an inch of the target. His second arrow split the branch right down the middle. Without giving Guy a chance to speak, Robin flung his bow aside and pulled out his sword. "Let that show you how little you know of archery, you villain!" he shouted. "Draw your sword, for I am Robin Hood!"

Guy stared at Robin for a moment in stunned surprise. Then he said angrily, "I am glad to meet you, Robin Hood," and snatched up his sword.

There followed the fiercest fight that Sherwood ever saw. Each man knew this was a battle to the death, and so they showed no mercy. Up and down the grass they fought, until the ground was crushed beneath their feet and their blood dripped on the earth.

Then Robin Hood jumped back from one of Guy's sword thrusts and caught his foot on a root. He fell heavily and Guy swung his sword at him with a shout of triumph. But Robin grabbed the blade in his bare hand and turned it aside. The blade slashed across his palm, drawing blood, but he was able to push Guy's sword into the ground. Then Robin leaped up and struck Guy with his sword. Guy cried out, then fell dead to the ground.

Robin Hood wiped the blood from his sword and walked over to where Guy of Gisbourne lay. "Today I have freed the world from an evil man," he said. "Since the Sheriff of Nottingham has sent this man against me, I will put on the fellow's clothes and see if I can pay back the Sheriff some of what I owe him from today's work."

Robin stripped off the bloody horse's hide from Guy's body and put in on himself. Then he drew the hood over his face so no one could see who he was and turned his steps toward Nottingham.

I think Robin got more than he bargained for this day! But what about Little John? Knowing him, I'm sure he's found some mischief—and a lot of trouble besides. Let's see what's happening to him!

15
Trouble for Little John

While Robin Hood was battling Guy of Gisbourne, Little John walked along the forest paths until he came to a cottage nestled among the trees at the side of the road. Here he stopped, for he thought he heard the sound of someone weeping. He knocked on the door and went in. Sitting by the fireplace was an old woman, rocking back and forth and crying bitterly.

Now Little John had a soft heart, so he sat down beside the woman, patted her on the shoulder to comfort her, and asked what was troubling her. "This morning I had three strong sons," the old woman said. "They were the finest men in Nottingham, and a great comfort to me since my husband died. Lately we have not had enough to eat, so my oldest son went out last night and shot one of the King's deer in the moonlight. The foresters followed the trail to this cottage and found the deer meat in the cupboard. Because neither of my younger sons would betray their brother, the foresters took all three away. The Sheriff is to hang them in Nottingham this very day!"

Little John was very moved by her story. "It is a terrible thing for the Sheriff to destroy a family just because they needed to feed themselves. I will do all I can to help you overcome this misfortune. I think there is a way I can save the lives of your three sons," Little John said. "Have you any clothes to lend me to wear in place of my Lincoln green so the Sheriff does not recognize me?"

The old widow found Little John some things to wear. In addition to the clothes, Little John took some sheep's wool and used it to make a wig and false beard. He placed these over his own dark hair and beard, and also put on a hat that had belonged to the widow's husband. Soon he was on his way to Nottingham in disguise, ready to rescue the widow's three sons.

Little John found the Sheriff and his men at an inn called the King's Head, just outside of Sherwood Forest. The widow's three sons were there as well, their hands bound behind their backs, waiting to be hanged for their crime.

"I will not hang these villains here, because I don't want to bring any bad luck upon this fine inn," the Sheriff said. "I will hang them on the very trees of Sherwood. That will show Robin Hood and his band of outlaws what they can expect of me if I ever catch them."

The three brothers fell on their knees and begged for mercy, but the Sheriff would not listen to a word they said. All this time, the disguised Little John stood to one side, watching and listening. The Sheriff spotted him and called him over, not realizing who the man really was.

"You look like a man who is big enough to take

care of these three. Would you like to earn sixpence today, my good fellow?" the Sheriff asked.

"Of course," Little John said. "I don't have enough money that I should pass up an offer of sixpence. What would you have me do?"

"These three men are to be hung," the Sheriff told him. "I don't want my soldiers to have to be hangmen. Will you string these men up to earn your sixpence?"

Little John agreed. "This is the perfect opportunity for me to save the lives of these three men," he said to himself. He walked behind the brothers to slip the nooses over their heads. "Never fear," he whispered into each brother's ear. "I am a friend of Robin Hood's, and I have come to help you." Then he cut the ropes binding the brothers' hands. "Run!" he shouted at them.

Before the Sheriff knew what had happened, the three men were racing into the woods with Little John right behind them. "You fool!" Little John shouted at the Sheriff. "I am Little John, and I would never help you kill three innocent men!"

The Sheriff realized he had been tricked. "That is one of Robin Hood's men!" he shouted. Overwhelmed with anger, he rode his horse right at Little John, swinging his sword. The flat of the blade caught Little John on the head and he fell to the ground, stunned.

When Little John woke up, he found himself tied hand and foot, a prisoner of the Sheriff. Then one of the Sheriff's men shouted, "Here comes Guy of

Gisbourne, the man you sent into the forest to kill Robin Hood!"

The Sheriff laughed and said to Little John, "See, my servant has killed your friend. Next I will kill you!"

Little John was filled with despair at the Sheriff's words. He could see the man walking toward them was carrying Robin Hood's bow and sword, and he thought his best friend was dead.

"What happened to you?" the Sheriff asked when Robin came closer. "Your clothes are covered with blood."

"If you don't like my clothes," said Robin in a harsh voice, "then close your eyes. This is the blood of the worst outlaw to ever set foot in the forest, the blood of the man I have killed today."

Little John could bear it no longer. "I don't care if you kill me," he told the Sheriff, tears running down his cheeks. "My life means nothing if Robin Hood is dead."

The Sheriff laughed, thinking he was rid of Robin at last. "What a good day this is turning out to be," he said. "Ask whatever you like of me, Guy of Gisbourne, and I shall give it to you."

"All I ask is that you give this man's life into my hands," Robin said.

The Sheriff thought this was a strange request, but he was happy to do it. He ordered his men to stand Little John against a tree and signaled Robin— whom the Sheriff thought was Guy of Gisbourne—to do what he liked to him.

Robin strung his bow, then walked up to Little John with his dagger in his hand. "Peace, my friend," he whispered in Little John's ear. "It is I, Robin Hood. When I cut your bonds, grab my sword and fight!"

Little John's heart leaped for joy when he realized his friend was not only alive but had come to rescue him. A huge grin spread over his face as Robin cut the ropes around Little John's wrists and ankles. The big man leaped forward and grabbed Robin's sword. Robin threw back the hood from his face and raised his bow and arrows. "Stand back!" he shouted.

"Robin Hood!" the Sheriff cried when he saw Robin's face. He was furious at being tricked again by his old enemy. He thought of fighting Robin on the spot, but he was too afraid.

Without another word, the Sheriff spurred his horse and rode toward Nottingham in a cloud of dust. His men were right behind him.

What an adventure! Robin battled the terrible Guy of Gisbourne, Little John saved the lives of three brothers, and then Robin saved the life of Little John! Yes sir, there was never a dull moment in Sherwood Forest....

16
Wedding in the Woods

One of the most often told stories of Robin Hood is the day he married his sweetheart, Maid Marian. After her father died, many cruel and powerful men wished to wed Marian—not because they loved her, but because they wanted her lands for themselves. Robin truly loved Marian, and he never forgot his promise to her. That was a magical day in Sherwood Forest....

The woods were hushed as Robin walked through the trees toward the clearing where his camp was. He was wearing his best suit of Lincoln green, for today was the day he would marry his sweetheart under the greenwood tree.

Robin's men were waiting for him in the clearing. They smiled joyfully as Robin walked past them, his head held high. At the front of the clearing, under the tree, stood Little John, who was to be Robin's best man that day. Friar Tuck stood beside him—he would perform the wedding ceremony. Both men grinned at Robin as he stepped up to them, but Robin barely glanced at his two friends. His eyes were set firmly on Marian.

Maid Marian waited for Robin under the tree with a smile on her face. She was wearing a simple gown of Lincoln green. Her hair hung loose down her back, and a wreath of wildflowers crowned her head. Robin thought she had never looked more beautiful.

Robin walked up to his love and they smiled at each other. Friar Tuck recited the simple words of the marriage ceremony. Then it was time for Robin and Marian to repeat the solemn vows that would make them forever man and wife.

"I, Robin, do take you, Marian, to be my wife, to have and to hold, to love and to cherish, in sickness and in health, for all the days of my life."

"I, Marian, do take you, Robin, to be my husband, to have and to hold, to love and to cherish, in sickness and in health, for all the days of my life."

"You may kiss the bride," Friar Tuck said, a smile crossing his face. Robin took Marian in his arms and kissed her gently.

"Hooray for Robin and Marian!" all the men shouted. They tossed their caps in the air and whistled so loudly that Robin and Marian began to laugh.

"Good for you, Robin!" Little John said, clapping his friend heartily on the back. "It's about time Marian joined us here in the woods. It's good for you two to be together at last."

"You are right, my friend," Robin said. He put his arm around Marian and hugged her.

"I have dreamed of this day for a long time," Marian whispered to Robin. "I am proud to be your wife."

All that day, the woods were filled with merrymaking. Robin's men had prepared a huge feast to celebrate his marriage. There were deer and chicken roasted over a fire, along with fresh bread and other delicious foods to eat. After the meal, the men entertained Robin and Marian with archery contests and other sports, and they also sang to the happy couple. The party lasted long into the night.

Robin and Marian were happy to be together, and happy to celebrate their marriage with all their friends. It was a day neither of them would ever forget.

17
King Richard of the Lion's Heart

Robin and Marian were now married, but Robin's adventures were not over. During this time, King Richard of the Lion's Heart had been captured in battle, and lay prisoner in a German castle. The Germans demanded a huge ransom to free the English King. The money to pay that ransom came from a tax that every person in England had to pay. So what did all this have to do with Robin Hood? Read on and see!

Robin was very upset at the thought of his King in a German prison. He thought of his own happy life and the freedom of the woods, then imagined King Richard locked up in a jail cell. To Robin, it seemed a terrible fate.

"I will do everything I can to free my King and bring him home to England," Robin said. So he gathered half of all the gold and silver that he and the Merry Men had collected and sent it to the mayor of London with a note that read, *From Robin Hood and his friends in Sherwood Forest, to free their beloved King.*

That wasn't the only thing Robin did to help King Richard. Whenever he heard of a wealthy man who refused to pay the tax to free the King, Robin paid the man a visit. He could usually convince the fellow to give his rightful share of the ransom— sometimes even more.

Word of Robin's efforts soon reached the ears of the King's treasurer. When King Richard was at last freed from prison, his treasurer told him all about Robin's work. "This man may love the King's deer," the treasurer said, "but it seems he loves his King even more."

"You say this man loves me," King Richard said, "yet I know he has given my Sheriff much trouble. How can someone be so loyal to his King, yet refuse to follow his laws? I would like to meet this unusual fellow."

King Richard could not stop thinking of the man who lived in Sherwood Forest. At last, he thought of a plan to find Robin Hood and test his faith. He called his five best knights to him and said, "We are going to ride into Sherwood Forest disguised as monks. We will load our horses with many riches to tempt the outlaws. Robin Hood and his men will not be able to resist trying to capture us!"

"Are you going to disguise yourself as well, Your Majesty?" one of the knights asked.

"Oh, yes," King Richard said. "If Robin Hood knows he is talking to the King, he will behave differently than if he thinks I am a monk. I want to see what this man is really like."

So King Richard and his men disguised themselves and traveled deep into Sherwood Forest. They rode for a long time, but they didn't see Robin or any of his men. Then King Richard stopped and said in a loud voice, "I wish I had a better head for remembering things. Here we have come all this way without a drop of anything to drink. I would give fifty pounds for something to quench my thirst."

No sooner had the King spoken than Robin Hood himself stepped out of the woods. "My friends keep a fine inn here in the forest," Robin told the King. "For fifty pounds, I can give you as noble a feast as you have ever tasted." He blew three notes on his horn, and a band of men in Lincoln green stepped out of the trees and surrounded the disguised men.

"Have you no respect for holy men such as we?" asked the King.

"Not a bit," Robin replied cheerfully. "Perhaps you've heard of me. My name is Robin Hood. I think you must be a very rich man to offer fifty pounds just for something to drink. Give me your purse, good friar, or I will have to take it from you myself."

"Here is my purse," said the King, handing his money pouch to Robin. "Lay not your lawless hands on me."

"You speak proud words," Robin said, laughing. "Are you the King of England to talk that way to me?" He took fifty pounds from the King's purse, then handed the rest back. "Here, my friend, I would not take everything you have. Push back your hood so I may see your face."

"No, I cannot," the King said, for he was afraid Robin might recognize him.

Robin shrugged. "Have it your way. Come along now, and join our merry feast!" He and his men led the King's company into the forest to the greenwood tree, where a great meal had been laid out on the grass.

Before anyone could start eating, Robin held his cup high and announced a toast. "Here's to good King Richard. May all his enemies be defeated!"

They all drank to the King's health, even the King himself. "I don't understand how outlaws such as you can honor the King with a toast," King Richard said to Robin.

"I tell you, those of us in Sherwood are more loyal to the King than anyone in the land," Robin said. "We would give up our very lives in his service."

Then Robin and his men entertained the King with many sports and games. There were archery contests and wrestling matches, and the woods were filled with shouting and laughter.

"I have not had such fun in many long days," King Richard announced.

Suddenly, Little John hurried into the clearing. With him were Robin's fair wife, Marian, and her uncle, Sir Richard of the Lea. "Robin, you must hurry to the safety of my castle!" Sir Richard shouted. "King

Richard himself has come to seek you in the woodlands." The knight stopped short when he saw Robin's guests. "Who are these men?" he asked.

"Just some friars who have joined me for a bite to eat," Robin said.

Sir Richard looked sharply at the King and his cheeks grew pale. The knight fell to his knees in respect, for he recognized his lord, the King of England.

Then the King threw back his hood and showed Robin and his friends who their guest really was. They all knelt down, too surprised to say a word.

King Richard looked at all the men. Finally, his gaze settled on Sir Richard of the Lea. "How dare you step between me and these fellows and offer your castle as a refuge for them," the King snapped. "Will you make your castle the hiding place for the most well-known outlaws in England?"

"I would never set out to anger Your Majesty," Sir Richard said bravely, "but I owe my life and my honor to Robin Hood. I cannot desert him in his hour of need."

King Richard nodded, for he admired loyalty more than anything else. Then he called Robin to him. "Three things have saved your life this day: my mercy, my love for a brave man, and the loyalty you have for me. I give you and all your men a full pardon, but I cannot let you roam the forest and break my laws as you have been doing. So I will take you at your word. You said that you and your men would give up your very lives in my service. Therefore, you, Little John, Will Scarlet, and Allan a Dale shall go back to London and join my household. Your wife, Marian, will also come to London with us. The rest of your men will become royal foresters. I would rather have them take care of Sherwood Forest than break my laws."

So it was that Robin, his wife, and his men entered King Richard's service. The next day, they all

rode into Nottingham with the King. The townspeople stared in wonder, for it was obvious that Robin Hood was high in the King's favor.

Robin Hood, Maid Marian, Little John, Will Scarlet, and Allan a Dale bid good-bye to their friends, promising to visit them in Sherwood whenever they could. Then they all rode off to have many more adventures in the company of the King.

What a tale! Robin Hood went into the King's service, taking Marian, Little John, Will Scarlet, and Allan a Dale with him. The rest of the Merry Men became the King's royal foresters, and they all continued to have many adventures...but those are stories for another day. This little dog has places to go and good deeds to do! See ya!